Kashner, Rita
The graceful exit

140009

MAUD PRESTON PALENSKE
MEMORIAL LIBRARY
St. Joseph, Michigan 49085
Tel. (616) 983-7167

THE GRACEFUL EXIT

ALSO BY RITA KASHNER

To the Tenth Generation 1984
Bed Rest 1981

THE
GRACEFUL
EXIT

RITA KASHNER

ATHENEUM • New York • 1989

This is a work of fiction. Names, characters, places, and incidents either are the product of the author's imagination or are used fictitiously. Any resemblance to actual events or persons, living or dead, is entirely coincidental.

Copyright © 1989 by Rita Kashner

All rights reserved. No part of this book may be reproduced or transmitted in any form or by any means, electronic or mechanical, including photocopying, recording, or by any information storage and retrieval system, without permission in writing from the Publisher.

Atheneum
Macmillan Publishing Company
866 Third Avenue, New York, N.Y. 10022
Collier Macmillan Canada, Inc.

Library of Congress Cataloging-in-Publication Data

Kashner, Rita.
    The graceful exit / Rita Kashner.
    p. cm.
    ISBN 0-689-12085-0
    I. Title.
PS3561.A6968G74   1989
813'.54—dc19   89-424   CIP

Designed by Helene Berinsky

10 9 8 7 6 5 4 3 2 1

Printed in the United States of America

For Pearl Marcus
Strength and dignity are her clothing,
And she laugheth at the time to come.

THE GRACEFUL EXIT

ONE

OH DEAR GOD. Morning again. *Monday* again. Caroline glowered nearsightedly at her quilt, focusing in on the sound. A voice. There wasn't supposed to be a voice, just music. The clock radio was across the room, a fiendish distance away, where she'd prudently set it last night. She threw her pillow at it. It didn't even muffle the voice, and now she was lying pillowless in a cold, hard world.

She snatched the quilt up over her head and waited for things to improve. She took a survey. Things weren't improving. She was still awake, it was still Monday morning, and the voice had been joined by another voice—a loud voice. The only way to stop the noise was to propel herself out of bed. To get vertical, cold, and in motion. Suffused with self-pity and wrapped in the quilt like an upright egg roll, she lurched toward the clock radio and savagely punched its soft-touch pad. The voices continued.

She looked suspiciously around the room. Nobody there, of course. Outside: it had to be coming from outside.

Clutching the quilt around her, she took a jerky series of baby steps over to the window, lifted one slat of the Levolors, and peered down. Four stories below, on the lawn in front of the building, were two men with hedgeclippers. One of them was talking loudly, aggrievedly, about his girlfriend. Ignoring her need to go to the bathroom, Caroline stood still and strained to catch his words until the whine of the hedge-cutters drowned them out.

Go to the bathroom, Caroline, she thought. *Get dressed and go sell some real estate. Who cares about this guy's love life?* But she was hooked; she pushed the blinds aside and cautiously stuck her head out the window, looking for the two men. They were rounding the corner of the building, rakes in hand. She dropped the quilt and ran to the window on the west side of the room. It was locked, of course. By the time she got it open, the men were too far away to be heard and she was shivering in the chilly April air. "Curiosity killed the cat," a flat voice echoed in her mind. Her mother in her lecturing mode. "One day, Miss, that nosiness will get you into A Situation."

"Oh, hi, Mom," she said out loud in the empty apartment. "Great to hear from you. I needed that this morning." And it wasn't until then that she remembered about her father. About how this was maybe the day to call the nice lady in Greenwich and meet her for lunch and arrange for Dad's premature demise. *That* Monday morning. O holy hopping hell.

■ ■ ■

Caroline, at the bathroom mirror, in solo catechism:

How are we going to get through this one?
We just will. Have to, that's all.
Who's going to get us through it?
Caroline Amelia Mayhew. And not another soul.

THE GRACEFUL EXIT

And what do we say?
Things will work out.
Skeptical green eyes looked back at her in the mirror.
Things will work out.
Deep breath, ready, set,
Launch.

TWO

SHE WAS THE first one in the office, as usual. She unlocked the doors, pushed open the one that said *REAL*, and went directly to her desk. Staring absently at the town map under the glass on her desktop, she willed things to come right: *He'll have changed his mind.* "Caroline, honey," he'll say, "how'd you like to make a little side trip to the body shop with me? Going to check myself back in, get fixed up once and for all."
She dialed his number.
"*Hay* lo."
"Hi, Dad."
"Hiya, Pickles. How's my girl?"
"Okay, fine. How'd the night go?" In automatic morning ritual, Caroline lined up the morning printout from the Multiple Home Listing Service, the local hotsheet, and the separate agencies' new listings. On the other side of her desk she made two piles: the morning's mail and her phone messages.
"The night went great. It's a true and genuine pleasure to pee alone, I want to tell you. And you know what else? Nobody in this whole apartment wants my blood."

THE GRACEFUL EXIT

"There's nobody there but you."

"You bet. Not a goddamn nurse in the joint."

"How do you feel?" She slit open the envelope from the photographer: portraits of two of her homes. One of them he'd managed to obscure almost entirely behind a bush. She stared glassily at the photos, waiting for her father's answer.

"I feel free, honey, and that feels good. I told you—I'd rather have a gut ache than stay in the hospital. I'd rather *die* of the gut ache than spend another day in that Transylvanian service station. If they don't kill you with their tests or bore you to death, they just go ahead and bleed you dry. Goddamn ghouls. Never again, Caroline."

"You told me."

"Meant it, too. Never again."

"All right. What will you do today?"

"Going to the club. Hey, you know who called me? Hal Minley. He said, 'Where you been keeping yourself?' I said, 'In the one place that makes you feel more like a fool than the golf course does.' He said, 'No kidding, you been hanging around the whorehouse?' " He laughed, a weak, thready laugh. Still, he sounded good. Coherent and positive. Still sober.

"You're not up to playing golf yet, are you?"

"No, but I'll ride around with them and kibitz." *And drink,* she thought, plummeting back into gloom, but she didn't say it. What she said was, "Have fun."

"Same to you, Pickles. Don't worry, either. I'm great."

"He's not doing so great," the doctor had told her last week, when she reached him from the pay phone in the hospital lounge.

"I know. But listen—"

"Your father is a difficult man, Caroline. A bright, charm-

5

ing, habitual heavy drinker—and he is in big trouble right now, which he is denying. Big trouble. Incipient gastric ulcers, enlarged heart, fatty liver. Any one of them could kill him; I told him that this morning. No sweet slipping away, either—three fine chances at a crappy, messy death."

"That's what you told him?"

"You bet. What should I have done? Danced around it? He has to be made to understand: his only chance is complete rest, simple diet, and total sobriety. The alternative is a year or so of misery—*misery*—and then good night nurse."

"Then that's why he's checking out."

"What?"

"He's paying his bill now."

"I see. Then he's going to have to find another doctor. I can't preside over it, you understand? I won't be responsible."

Standing there focusing on the change she'd lined up on the ledge in the phone booth, Caroline had said nothing, but she had made the decision: *Then I will.* Now, on a Monday morning in April, looking at the streets intersecting at odd angles on her town map, she picked up the phone and made the date for lunch. Then she cried. Then she called her banker and sold a CD.

Then she called her oldest friend, Janet, and told her she'd made the lunch date. There was a reverent silence, a rare response for Janet. It went on two beats too long. Three.

"Janet?" Caroline demanded finally.

"I don't know what to say."

"I'm canceling. I'm calling her now. Hang up."

"No! You can't cancel! It's just—"

"What?"

"Give me a minute, will you? What would you say to me if I told you I was having lunch in Westport with a Smith

alumna who was going to take out a contract on my father's life?"
"I'd say you were wasting money. Your father's dead."
Nobody said anything for a minute. Caroline spoke first.
"I'm sorry," she said.
"Don't be silly. It's not news to me; he's been dead every day for six years. I just . . . I guess I didn't expect you to go through with it. And so fast—you called her just now, and she's meeting you for lunch?"
"I guess it's her slow season," Caroline said sulkily. "She had no other patricides lined up for today."
"You know what?" Janet was recovering. "It's good. You won't have to sit around thinking about it. Go for it, honey. What choice do you have?"
"I'm a wreck."
"Of course."
"Should I bring cash?"
"What, to the Petite Auberge in Westport? What're you going to do, pass it to her in a rolled-up *Vogue*? Jesus, I told you, Stephie met her at a Smith luncheon. She's like us, Caroline."
"Well, not quite."
"How long have you and I known each other?"
"Since second grade. So?"
"So am I going to let you go to some gangster? Stephie said she was wonderful. Very understanding, actually. Very caring."
"Except the part where she—"
"It's up to you."
"I hate when you say that. I've always hated it when you said that. You make me—"
"Caroline, go and meet her. Do not bring cash. Bring Kleenex, and for Chrissake don't get lost. You turn just after—"
"I *know*. You told me. I'll be fine. I'm not going to get lost

and I'm not going to cry. I never cry in front of anybody."
"I know. Don't start now."
"I won't."

She missed the turn and drove around in frantic zigzags, finally asking someone the way and arriving fifteen minutes late and out of breath. Pulling down the sun visor she peered into the car mirror. Her cheeks were flushed. She ran a brush through her hair, which crackled with static and floated up in a dark nimbus around its smooth bob. Her bangs were damp, sticking to her forehead in spikes. She swiped at them with the end of her scarf and hastily brushed them smooth. She looked into her own eyes. "Oh boy," she breathed. Then she launched herself out of the car and ran up the graveled driveway to the restaurant. *She'll be gone,* Caroline prayed, but when she gave the maître d' her name, he led her directly to a table. The woman looked up and smiled. Elegant. Pretty. Controlled. *Well, she would be controlled,* Caroline thought, and held out her hand.

"I'm Caroline Mayhew," she said. "So sorry I'm late."

"Don't worry. The traffic on Route One is getting very bad lately. Come sit down and catch your breath. My name is Margaret."

"Oh. No last names, right?"

"Well, I'd eventually need to have your full name, of course."

"Right, right."

"But my professional name is simply Margaret."

"I understand."

A waiter appeared, a dark-haired young man wearing black trousers, a white shirt and a red bow tie. "Ah, your friend has arrived," he said. "How are you ladies this afternoon?"

"Very well, thank you, Christopher."

THE GRACEFUL EXIT

Margaret's voice was low and well modulated, just the right mixture of pleasantry and command. A faint note of Miss Porter's School in the pronunciation. Caroline, registering it, relaxed a bit.

"May I offer you something from the bar? Perhaps a glass of one of our very nice California wines?"

He was looking at Caroline; she was going to have to declare herself first. *I ought to stick to Perrier*, she thought, and said, "Vodka gimlet, please. Straight up." *Good going, Caroline. A lot of control there.* She had landed in the booth half sitting on her raincoat. She put her handbag down and stood to fold the coat, Burberry plaid out, and laid it on the banquette next to her. "Evian water and a slice of lime, please," she heard Margaret say as she sank back into her seat, narrowly missing her handbag.

Margaret was sitting in Zenlike stillness, a serene and accepting half smile in her eyes. She was a pretty blonde with even, smooth skin and good cheekbones. Her hair was pulled back into a bun. Tiny gold love knot earrings. White wool suit, pale gray linen blouse. Very good pearls. Cartier watch. The woman represented a major investment in quiet elegance. *She must have had a good year,* Caroline thought. *I'm not the only patricide in town.*

"I got your name—" Caroline began, but Margaret said, "Ah, Christopher, that was very quick," as the waiter reappeared with their drinks. He listed seven specialties of the day in theatrical cadence. Caroline cocked her head as if she were listening raptly, only really beginning to focus halfway through the recitation. " . . . tiny spinach tortellini in our sauce Alfredo with medallions of lobster," he was saying. "Calves liver Bordelaise, garnished with whole baby carrots and our julienne of beets and yarrow root. Salad of smoked duckling . . . "

"The last thing I want is liver," Caroline joked feebly when

9

he'd left with their orders. Margaret blinked politely, still smiling, waiting to hear why. "Well, you know, my father . . . his liver . . . that's the whole *problem*, that's why—"

Margaret raised just her fingertips off the table and smiled a firm warning at Caroline, to stop her. She had healthy, pink nails with white oval tips, all the same length. "I think it's best if we wait to discuss business," she cautioned.

"Oh, I wasn't—"

"I know. But do feel free to tell me about your father. His likes and dislikes, that sort of thing. Hobbies. Dreams. You're very close?"

"Drinkers are very open people, you know. I mean, that's the nice thing about them. They talk and they listen, unless they're really far gone. He does, anyway. I used to sit with him when he had his scotch before dinner. Scotches. Mother'd be banging things around in the kitchen and he'd be telling me about this contract he was working on, or something funny he'd heard and what it made him think of. I'd tell him things that were going on with me, and he . . . the thing is, he never *judged*, you know?"

Margaret frowned in sympathy, nodding slowly.

"So yes, we're close. I mean, now it's hard sometimes. Often. He's—well, he's feeling pretty lousy a lot of the time. And his mind gets caught in this loop, so that he tries to tell you something and goes around and around three or four times until he gets frustrated, or you do. But a lot of the time he's his old self . . . "

"It's hard."

"It's very hard."

"Don't worry, Caroline. We're going to help you."

They drove the fifteen minutes to Greenwich in Margaret's car. "It's best if there aren't a lot of strange cars going in and out of the driveway," she explained. It was a large split ranch, set way back on the land. Slate roof, fieldstone walls, good plantings, in-ground sprinkler system. Well built, impeccably maintained. Caroline priced it automatically: a self-seller, perfect for a law partner or investment banker. They went around back to the garden and down three steps to the office, a sunny room with a white tile floor, a pastel Oriental rug, a plump couch covered in a peach and lavender chintz, and peach and lavender pillows on wicker chairs. In front of the couch was a coffee table strewn with magazines and pamphlets. "Have a look while I get us some iced tea," Margaret said.

The magazines—*Town & Country, Connoisseur, Harper's, Travel & Leisure*—were open to travel and entertainment articles. There were travel folders, not the trifold glossy kind that sit in racks in travel agencies but offerings on heavy stock, small booklets about lush retreats or individually conducted tours and cruises. There was a robin's-egg blue Tiffany catalogue and one from Cartier's.

"That's an old one," Margaret said, returning with a tray. "We have the current catalog. But I don't think you want—"

"No."

"We do a lot with yacht charters for our older men."

"No—"

"And any kind of activity or event you can think of. We had a gentleman once, all he wanted in life was to conduct a symphony orchestra. Stravinsky, can you imagine?"

"Tch."

"We booked him a year of private lessons with a very well-known conductor—"

"A year! I don't—"

"No, no, of course not. This was a very special case. He had time. Just. Anyway, we got him the Salt Lake City Philharmonic, a private gala—"

11

"Wow."

"You bet. Cocktails before, black-tie dinner after for three hundred and fifty people, and he conducted that orchestra in Stravinsky's *Rite of Spring*. He was just ecstatic."

"Too bad he had to die to get to do it."

Margaret frowned. "Our service at Great Events is to provide the peak moment, Caroline." She pronounced the word reverentially, as though it had a capital *M*. "It's *all* we provide. I hope you understand that."

"Oh, I didn't mean—but you do *know* someone? I mean you recommend—"

"Shall we take this from the beginning?"

"All right."

"Your father is very ill. Cirrhosis, I gather?"

"Yes. And other things."

"And his capacities are becoming . . . diminished?"

Caroline nodded.

"And you would like him to have a very special experience. A lifetime high, something he's dreamed of but never dreamed would happen."

"Yes."

"And then never to be ill or . . . diminishing again."

"Look, I want you to understand—"

"It's because you love him."

Caroline nodded again.

"I know. Believe me, you're not the only one. If you could see my waiting list. People desperate—"

"Oh, listen, I'm very grateful that you could—"

"I never turn away anyone with an alcoholic parent. It's the one indulgence I allow myself. Personal reasons. A quiet crusade, if you like." Caroline suddenly envisioned Margaret as a blond, impeccably tailored Joan of Arc, leading an army of alcoholics into a sort of celestial Disneyland. "And incidentally," Margaret went on, "alcoholics are among the best

Beneficiaries we have, because they usually *are* outgoing people. They enjoy their Moments so wholeheartedly. It gives us a great deal of satisfaction."

"Do you—are you *there* for the, uh, Moment? I mean, how do you know?"

"Oh, no, we're never present. We couldn't possibly be. Our Moments take place all over the world, for one thing: I'd never get any work done. And then some are very private events, you know. We simply don't belong there. But we hear from their loved ones, of course—afterward. Or, if it's inappropriate for *them* to be there, often there are photos or videotapes. We have marvelous photo and video people. Or, failing that, we have the reports that come in from our Enhancement Staff."

"Your . . . ?"

"We have a very special file of people. We can arrange almost anything, Caroline. What you see on the table here represents just the very obvious possibilities. Any travel agent can book a tour. But a weekend with royalty? A special proclamation in Congress? Chess with a master? And we have access to world-class instructors in anything you can name. Fashion designers. Celebrities. Actors and actresses, of course, as well. If you know what you want for your father, we can make it happen, or we can create the illusion. If you don't know what you want, we can help you to arrive at just the—"

"The once-in-a-lifetime event."

"Yes. So, tell me about your father. What's his name, first of all?"

"Charlie. Charles Joseph Mayhew."

"Hobbies?"

"Aside from drinking?"

"Of course."

"Well, he used to play bridge, before Mother left him. And

golf, of course. He played golf for Princeton, a hundred years ago. He still plays twice a week. It's about all he does, anymore."

Margaret narrowed her eyes, thinking. "Golf," she whispered. "Bridge. What if . . . no. Wait! How about a week at St. Andrews in Scotland? The Royal and Ancient Golf Club." She rolled the words admiringly, then paused in thought. "For a moment there I was thinking Pebble Beach, with perhaps a long sunset cocktail hour at San Simeon, Clint Eastwood giving him the keys . . . but that's not really his style, is it?"

"No."

"No. St. Andrews. Knickers, his oldest argyles. Gorse. Bridge at the Duke and Duchess's on Wednesday evening. Get that fellow . . . what's his name . . . " She got up and opened a lavender lacquered file cabinet and extracted a folder. She sat down again, leafed through the folder's contents, put it down exasperatedly and got another folder out of the cabinet, after some searching. "Aha. Brian MacCloud. The ultimate caddy. He'll caddy exclusively for your father for the week. Quite a bully, I understand, but simply the best." She stared into the middle distance for a moment. "I wonder if we couldn't get Jack Nicklaus to go eighteen holes with him midweek. Private instruction, you know?"

"He'd die for that! Oh my God." Caroline clapped a hand to her mouth. Then, composing herself, she folded her hands in her lap and leaned forward. "Whatever it takes, I can pay for it."

"I know. It's a question of availability, of course."

"Of course."

Still perusing the contents of the folder, Margaret said, "I'll put a call in to Texas . . . best custom-made clubs in the world. Graphite shafts, I think. It will take them at least six weeks to make them—but then it has to be six weeks, even without the clubs: this is April, and the season doesn't begin until May, in Scotland. Matter of fact, we're best off waiting for late May. It's lovely there then." She looked directly at Caroline. "Do we have six weeks?"

"I think so. He's just come out of the hospital, so he's detoxed. And if he's busy and excited . . . "

"Oh, we'll keep him both busy and excited, I promise you. How about filling in the time with some lessons? I can arrange for him to work with the pro down at Baltusrol for a month, while he's waiting for the clubs. Kind of gear him up for St. Andrews. What do you think?"

"Well, he doesn't always show up for appointments."

"Oh, that would be okay at Baltusrol—whatever practice time he got in would be fine. This is not the PGA, after all. But could someone accompany him to Texas for the fittings?"

"Fittings?"

"Weight, flexibility of shaft and so on. These are custom clubs. Of course, we could fly the engineer here from Texas, but part of the experience is to be there in the shop, choose the woods, talk technicalities with the guys—"

"He'd love it. I'll try to free up the time."

"All right! This is coming together! Wait, you know what else? Hold on . . . " She jumped up, opened a drawer, and began thumbing through files. "Let's see . . . Romerbad, Scotland, Sotogrande, Turnberry . . . Whiskey! Here we go. Ewen MacPherran. This fellow has a castle in the north. Lovely old Scot. In the basement of the castle, like the Cask of Amontillado, he has barrel upon barrel of rare old whiskeys, the kind the brewers put away and never sell. Come to think of it, I wonder how he gets them. Ambrosial, really. He once told me, 'When my time comes, I want tae sip frae here and sip frae there, frae the dawn tae the dark. And then I'll choose a barrel, lift oop the lid, and slide on in. I'll die drownin' in the rivers of the gods and they'll never have tae bury me at all. I'll be pickled in the best there is.' " She smiled reminiscently. "He's not your average Scot. Chatty, open, cheerful. I think he'd be a great drinking companion."

"But Dad couldn't drink that much and play St. Andrews."

"No. But *after* St. Andrews, full of the pleasure of his new clubs and the course and the evening of bridge, he could go and spend this one last day and evening with Ewen at the castle." Margaret was flushed with benevolence.

"Oh."

"A long sunset, so to speak."

"In the cellar."

"That bothers you. All right, let's think—"

"No, I didn't mean that. I just . . . but of course that's just how he'd want it. And he wouldn't be alone?"

"No. Our friendly Scot would match him snort for snort right through the evening. Right up to the end. Look, you think about it. I'll leave you here with the material on St. Andrews—"

"No! Don't go! I mean, it's fine. More than fine. It's wonderful, really. He would choose it if—"

"If he dreamed he could."

"Yes. And I'll free the time for Texas and so on."

They sat in silence for a moment. Then Margaret took a pad of paper off her desk and began to write. "Texas for the custom clubs," she read off softly, "then a few weeks at Baltusrol; call the pro. St. Andrews: Brian MacCloud to caddy; get Edwina to talk to the Duchess about Wednesday bridge. No, I'll call her myself. Nicklaus . . . I'll have to think about how to do that. And Ewen and his whiskey." She looked up and smiled. "It's delightful, you know? Just the right balance."

"But then . . . I mean how . . . " Caroline looked pleadingly at Margaret, but no help came. The woman had the most unnerving capacity for sitting still and waiting. "There has to be . . . we haven't talked about . . ." Still no help. "Will he be pushed into a barrel of rye, or what?" Caroline finally blurted.

Margaret's eyebrows went up. Then she sighed. "Why would poor old Ewen do that?" she inquired.

"Then how . . . I mean, you said . . . I thought it was understood . . ."

"We arrange for, as you put it, a once-in-a-lifetime experience. That's all we do; you must clearly understand that."

"But—?"

"Do you? Caroline?"

"Yes—"

"Then, with that clearly understood, I will ask you: were you thinking of speaking with a doctor regarding your father's condition?"

"Speaking with . . . Oh. Okay. I mean, yes, I was."

"I make no recommendations and I make no arrangements with any doctor. You understand that."

Caroline was listening very carefully. She nodded.

"But if you would like, as a friend, I can give you the phone number of a specialist who is said to be knowledgeable and capable."

"All right. Uh, when will that be?"

"Now, if you like. Or never. I can simply make the arrangements for this lovely treat, round-trip ticket, confirmed return."

"No. Return to what?"

Margaret nodded slowly in sympathy, then stood up. "Come with me. I know you'd like some privacy for your consultation." Caroline followed her out of the room, through a hallway, and into a smaller room. It was a library, paneled in lustrous old wood—must have been imported; this house was 1956 at the earliest—and furnished in chintzes and a dark Oriental rug. Margaret gestured to a built-in wet bar in the corner. "Anything you'd like. Please help yourself. Or—look, I can"—she opened a drawer, then another, then a small cabinet—"Aha"—from which she produced a small prescription cylinder. Valium; Caroline recognized the yellow pills from the days of her marriage. She shook her head. "I don't need that. Thanks. I might have a drink, though."

"Of course. And anytime you're ready, just sit yourself down in that chair." It was an oversized wing chair, wine-colored leather edged with brass studs. Behind it was a small tambour desk with a telephone on it, and a box of Kleenex. "The chair swivels," Margaret said. "Use this number. Oh, and Caroline? Talk as long as you like, and try to get all your questions answered during this conversation. If you need to contact the doctor again you can, of course, but you'll have to trot all the way back here to do it. It's a nuisance, but the phone number does change quite often and I can't give it to you unless you're here."

Caroline nodded, eyes on the phone.

"I'll just leave you alone now. When you're ready, come on back to the office. I'll have started making your calls. It's early afternoon in Texas. Don't worry about running into anyone else here, incidentally. That will never happen." She was gone, leaving her serene smile shimmering in the room like the Cheshire cat's. The door closed solidly behind her.

Caroline poured herself a vodka and tonic. There were fresh flowers in a brass bowl on the bar, and a small basket of limes and lemons with an ivory-handled knife. "Have a drink, Caroline," she said softly. Glass in hand, she crossed the room and sank into the wing chair. "Hello, Central, give me Euthanasia five-oh-two," she muttered. "Dr. Borgia? I'd like to make an appointment to do Daddy in."

She swiveled the chair so that she was secluded, facing rows of books. "*Lives of the Great Poisoners*," she said darkly. She sat her drink down on the little desk, then picked it back up and took a swallow. She replaced it on its coaster, leaned forward, placed her feet on the floor, and dialed the number. It was picked up after a ring and a half. "This is Dr. Gray," a pleasant voice said. "How can I help?"

"My father—his liver. He, um, drinks, and the doctor, the *other* doctor, the internist said—"

"Yes. Tell me what he said. Take your time. Take a deep breath."

She took a swig of vodka and tonic. "He gave up the case, actually, when my father checked himself out of the hospital against his advice. He said—he said a year of misery . . . three messy, awful deaths." She covered the mouthpiece and blew her nose.

"Surely not three? We each of us get but one, as far as I know. Are we helpless in the face of suffering and humiliation, or do we choose our moment, that's the question."

"I'm choosing for him."

"An act of courage, uh—may I ask your name?"

"Caroline."

"An act of courage, Caroline. And of love. Now tell me: You've decided upon a peak experience for your father?"

"Uh-huh."

"And where will that be?"

"In a cellar in Scotland, with Ewen MacSomebody and his barrels." She was getting tipsy, she suddenly realized. Good. She drained the glass, blew her nose again, took off her shoes, pulled her legs up under her in the chair and leaned against the deep leather wing.

"Would you like to tell me about his Moment?"

She told him, in as orderly a fashion as she could manage, interrupting herself between Baltusrol and St. Andrews. "Could you hang on a second? Just—I want to get something. Is it okay?"

"Go right ahead."

She made her way to the bar again and mixed another drink. "Have yourself another drink, Caroline," she muttered. "Fitting occasion." By the time she regained the chair, she'd sipped off the top third of the drink. She arranged herself carefully within the chair again.

"I'm back," she said into the phone. "Dr. Black?"

"Gray. Yes, Caroline, I'm right here. You were telling me about Scotland."

"Whole lot of golf. Nine holes forward, same nine backward. The Royal and Ancient." She outlined the rest of it raggedly, ending with Ewen and his barrels.

"Lovely. Ah, lovely. What an indulgence. What a caring, generous thing you're doing for your father."

"Yes, but how am I doing it? I mean how do we . . . you . . . at the end, who—"

"Ah, that's my contribution. I attend to it personally. My specialty is in thanatology, you know. And you're not to worry: I never miss, and there's never a moment's pain or fear. I promise you that. They go to sleep, that's all. A gentle sleep after their most cherished dream has been fulfilled. And it makes for a beautiful final image, incidentally, if there's to be an open casket. No distortion or discoloration at all."

She swallowed the rest of the drink. "Uh-huh."

"No residue, no need for alarm or suspicion. Just—"

"Good night nurse."

"Good night world."

"I don't suppose you take MasterCard."

He chuckled appreciatively. "No, we deal strictly in cash. Safest for you, actually. But don't worry about that. My work is billed to you through Margaret."

"Payable upon satisfaction?" She was sounding snappish, she realized repentantly. No reason to blame the doctor.

"You'll have to ask Margaret about that end of things." His voice hadn't wavered from its tone of warm concern.

THE GRACEFUL EXIT

"What I'd like you to focus on is the richness of those last days, and the ease of the slipping away, Caroline. Cirrhosis, or esophageal bleeding—the choking and the terror, the terrible pain, the loss of control—why should he go through that? When he can play out his final days pampered, cheerful, triumphant and delighted at every turn."

"I know. It's better."

"Far better. I take it as a privilege to be able to help."

She blew her nose. "Don't hurt him."

"I promised you—no pain."

"Okay. Thank you, then."

"Good-bye, Caroline. Remember, richness, triumph, cheer, and an easy parting."

"Okay. Bye."

"Huh." She sat in the chair another moment, staring ahead, then she found her shoes and put them on, stood, hiked up her skirt and pulled her sweater straight, returned the empty glass to the bar, and went to find Margaret.

She found a bathroom instead, and then a laundry, before she turned herself around and located the office. Margaret, who was on the phone, made an O with her thumb and index finger and then waved Caroline to the couch. Her desk was piled with folders now, and there was a scattering of notes and brochures on top of the folders. Caroline caught sight of herself in a tiled mirror behind the desk. She was flushed, and her eyes were dark and too bright.

"He'll be charmed and honored to be included, Your Ladyship," Margaret shouted into the phone. "You really are too wicked to tempt me ... no, no, to *tempt* me, but I can't possibly. Just my old friend Charlie Mayhew, this time. I'll be by in the fall, though ... the *fall*, October, and I'll bring you those cuttings. I'll smuggle them in. ... Absolutely. Count on it. ... Yes. Good-bye." She hung up the phone. "Hah!"

"Good news?"

"Fantastic. The clubs in twenty-one days—not a full range of the African woods to choose from at such short notice, but a good assortment available. Guest privileges at Baltusrol all arranged, *and* bridge with the Duke and Duchess. All subject to your final approval, of course. And I have somebody working on Brian MacCloud. It's going to work, Caroline!"

"What time is it in Scotland?"

"Nine-thirty. We won't hear about MacCloud tonight, but I'm working on a fantastic hotel booking . . . Caroline?"

She was asleep.

THREE

SHE WOKE UP when the doorbell rang. Someone had draped a soft mohair throw over her while she slept, and now a woman approached, tossed a corner of the throw loosely over her face, and whispered urgently, "So sorry, Caroline; I'll get her out of here in a minute. This *never* happens."

. . . Margaret. Doing Daddy in. Dr. Black. But why was this blanket over her face? Oh, of course; to protect her identity. I'm undercover, she told herself with foggy hilarity. Wishing for a glass of cold water, she pulled the throw farther over her head, exposing her feet, and lay still as death.

"Libby, dear, I've explained that you make things awkward when you simply arrive here like this. You don't want to run into any—"

"I know, I know. But it's late and I thought no one would be here—"

"Someone is, actually."

"Whoops. But—oh, I see. Jesus, is she dead?"

"Certainly not. She's exhausted, and I'm working on some West Coast calls for her. So perhaps tomorrow or Wednesday—"

"No, listen, I'll be just a minute." The woman's voice lowered; it was barely audible now. Caroline peered in vain through the peachy mohair, and listened hard. "It's about Mother again. I thought about it and I definitely don't want to dump her in the sea. I mean, she adored Hilton Head and all that, but she never actually *swam*. I was going to do it, you know. I hired this adorable seaplane—five hundred dollars for forty-five minutes, and the minister and I could go along—and I was all set to go out beyond the breakwater at Saybrook and scatter the ashes, but then I thought, why get her wet *now*?"

"Then how about over the house in Garrison?"

"Are you kidding? That's where Father's been living with the new wife. Eleanor. Scatter Mother there so that cow can dust her off the front porch?"

"Hm. Well, what was her favorite place?"

"Fifty-seventh, between Fifth and Madison. Actually, I thought of putting her in the plantings in Trump Tower, but that was the whole point, wasn't it? Not to put her in the dirt?" She paused a moment, then said thoughtfully, "I could put her in the safety-deposit box, couldn't I?"

"I suppose. Look, Libby—"

"She'd love it in there with the jewels. I looked in the canister, incidentally, and the ashes are in a plastic bag, no bigger than this."

Lie still, Caroline reminded herself; she desperately wanted to peek out and see Libby, and to learn how big a plastic bag Mother's remains required.

"So I could definitely fit her in the vault, where the pearls and the brooch and things are. I'm glad I paid the extra seventy-five dollars for pulverization, because—"

"Perfect. Libby, the vault is perfect. What could be safer? And it's quiet, dry—"

"Temperature controlled."
"Absolutely. She'd be pleased."
"Nothing pleased Mother. Except good jewelry, of course."
"Just one quick thing: don't carry the canister into the bank as it is. Someone might recognize what it is, and there may be health laws. Use a tote bag or something."
"She's got her own. She fits perfectly into the small Hermès lizard tote."
"Good. Do it tomorrow; it'll set your mind at ease. And do let me know—but over the phone, Libby."
"I know. Privacy and anonymity."
"Yours as well as others'."
"Okey-doke. Toodle!"
"Good luck."

The door closed and Caroline heard a bolt click. "All clear," Margaret said after a moment. "Caroline, I'm so sorry. In fact I'm sorry I ever took this case. She's driving me berserk. Do you know, she's been riding around with that canister for four months? She can't make up her mind about what to do with her mother's ashes, and every time she comes up with an idea about their disposal she calls to see what I think about it."

"She keeps her mother's ashes in the car?"

"In the trunk of her Volvo. I rode with her once, just after her mother's Moment. She'd come to a pothole and she'd sing out, 'Look out, Mother, here comes a bump!' "

"Weird."

"You don't know the half of it. But she should never have appeared here like that. She knows the rules. Are you all right?"

"Sure. I can't believe I fell asleep. What time is it?"

"Five-fifteen."

"Oh, how awful. I'm sorry."

"Don't worry. I always work until seven or so. This is the best time for getting things done. In fact, your project is coming along incredibly well. Would you like a progress report?"

"Well, I—if you don't mind, I seem to be a little fuzzy now. Is it all right if I call tomorrow?"

"Why don't you come in, let's see . . . the day after tomorrow? I have the Alzheimer's luncheon tomorrow, but Wednesday looks good. Say eleven or so? I have no appointments at all that day, and the details should have fallen into place by then."

"You work fast."

"My clients expect that. By the time they come to me, time is definitely an element."

"You see a lot of grief."

"I see everything."

In Margaret's car, on the way to the parking lot of the Petite Auberge, Caroline ventured, "What arrangements would you like to make for, uh, payment? I mean, on Wednesday I could bring—"

"Unmarked bills?" Margaret smiled. "No need for that. Many of my clients prefer to pay in cash for their own reasons, but I accept checks, American Express, MasterCard, whatever is convenient for you." She pulled up alongside Caroline's car. "It's kind of late. I hope no one was expecting you earlier?"

"No. No problem."

On the way home, she figured out how long it had been since anyone had been expecting her: two years, one month, and seventeen days. She missed the turn onto the highway and found herself on a winding road, driving deeper and deeper into a residential area. Just before she decided to turn around, she saw a dip in the road ahead. "Look out, Dad," she said out loud in the empty car, "here comes a bump."

"But I didn't cry," she reported to Janet that night. "At least not where she could see me."

"Good going. What's she like?"

"Beautiful."

"You think everybody's beautiful."

"No, really. Blond, elegant, no hips, great cheekbones . . . and really pulled together. In her whole life, this woman has never dropped an ice cream cone."

"Madame Defarge never dropped a stitch. It's hardly grounds for enshrinement."

"No, she's really nice. I mean, think about all the pain she absorbs every day. They're both really nice, her and Dr. Death. Except her files are a mess."

"Caroline—"

"No, you should see it. Nothing's where she expects it to be, and within two hours she had files falling off her desk, little notes flying around all over the place. She had to look in three places before she found the Valium."

"She popped one while you were there? Real pulled together."

"No, it was for me. She offered me one before I made the phone call."

"You take it?"

"Of course not. I haven't had one since—"

"I know. Since Peter the Sailor Man took his leave. Listen to me, Caroline: you are not to lay one hand on those files. It's not your job to straighten out her life. Can you remember that?"

"Of course. Anyway, what do you think I'm going to do?"

"What you always do: try to fix it all up. You have to hear

yourself— '... all the pain she absorbs ... files a mess ... can't find the Valium.' You're getting ready to move in there and do your Little Mary Sunshine bit. And I'm telling you—"

"Janet."

"What?"

"I'm hanging up now. I'll call you tomorrow; you can tell me then."

"I will."

"I know."

She was annoyed at Janet and a little worried because she'd hung up on her. But Janet hung up on her all the time; a third of their conversations ended that way, and had since they were seven. Caroline was restless. She wanted to do something carefree, and for a minute she stood looking out the window, trying to think what that would be. Then she turned on her answering machine, picked up messages from three current clients and one old one, put on her happy voice, and began returning the calls.

Her A.M. appointment was to show a house on a second visit. The clients were a young couple buying their first home. They'd fallen in love with a three-bedroom Colonial with a Japanese maple in the front yard, and the young woman wanted her father to see the house. He was involved in construction somehow—they didn't say how, but the two of them took an hour to go through the house, peering at beams in the attic and conferring earnestly, in low voices, over the furnace and hot-water heater. Finally they went out to the back yard and stood facing the house, the father making broad, geometric gestures with his arms: a patio here, a door there, leading outside from the family room; you could expand out here, make the kitchen bigger. Caroline stood unobtrusively in the kitchen, watching them. She'd seen the gestures a hundred times. She could read them like sign language: they meant a sale. The young woman's expression changed from intense concentration to the glow of acquisition; her father smiled indulgently. They agreed: this is the house.

Caroline returned to her office at eleven o'clock and phoned in the client's offer, still warmed by the tableau. The young woman's father had been robust, fit; he moved with the carelessness of the healthy. He was brisk and decisive. His daughter nodded solemnly when he spoke. She relied on him. Caroline dialed her father's number.

"Dad?"

"Hi."

"Did I wake you?"

"No, no. How are ya? Feeling good?"

"Fine, Dad. How about you? How was the club?" There was a pause. "Dad?"

"Great. Great." He cleared his throat. "Nice to see everybody. Nice to see *anybody*, after that hole."

"You sound tired."

"Well, hell, they drained out my blood, you know. I'm running about three quarts low. How's—did you sell a couple houses today?"

"I have one that looks good."

"Fine. That's fine."

"What are you doing today? Got plans?"

"Oh, sure. I'll be busy. One thing and another. See the ... uh ... the paper. Go over to the club. Little shopping."

"Don't forget to eat."

"Don't worry. I'm doing great."

"Okay, Dad. Take care."

"Live it up, Pickles. My advice."

She held her finger on the disconnect button and looked at the receiver in her hand, thinking about Dr. Death and his caring, gentle voice. "If Simon calls tonight, I'm going to see him," she told the receiver grimly. "Mustache or no." Then she hung it up.

Simon called at nine forty-five. She was already in her robe and slippers. "Hi," he said almost inaudibly. "How've you been?"

"Why are you whispering?"

"The kids are here. It's my week."

"Simon, sometime they're going to have to know that you're dating."

"I know. They're just not ready."

"They know that their mother's seeing someone, don't they?"

"Sure. And Justin wets the bed every night. They have to have some stability somewhere."

"They seemed to like me all right when I ran into the three of you at the flea market."

" . . . Yes. Well, they just need time. Meanwhile, I have to live with the split . . . on one hand, my commitment to them; on the other"—he must have put his mouth right against the phone; the words suddenly leapt, intimate and distorted, into her ear—"certain very sweet adult pleasures with a certain delicious lady."

The picture materialized in her mind: Simon groping upward for her in the half dark of his stark bedroom, his face a mask, his eyes and the mustache dark cutouts. She sighed.

"Are you blushing?" he hissed. "I love it when there's a blush on that white Irish skin of yours."

"I don't know; I can't see myself." She was whispering, too, idiotically. And lying: she was definitely not blushing. She doodled ferociously on the message pad near the phone. Why didn't she just say it: *No, Simon, I'm not blushing. I'm picturing your stupid mustache and I'm wondering why the orthodontist didn't fix that hiss when he straightened your overbite.*

Instead, she let him think she was going all swoony over his moist, clandestine mating calls.

"Wish I could see through the phone," he breathed. "You blush in all kinds of interesting places. Are we set for Saturday?"

"What about your kids?"

"Ellen has them. Her week begins Saturday at ten. I'll pick you up at noon?"

"Sure. Good night, Simon."

"Good night till Saturday"—the voice had zeroed in again, sibilant and exaggerated—"sweet lady."

F_OUR_

MARGARET PICKED HER up at the Petite Auberge at eleven on Wednesday.

"How was your Alzheimer's luncheon?" Caroline asked.

"Well, depressing, of course."

"Annual fund-raiser?"

"No, no. This is a group of children and spouses of Alzheimer victims—women mostly, of course. They meet monthly with a social worker and a gerontologist—lunch and commiseration. Do you know, there were seven of them when they started and now there are nearly fifty? A lot of them with early-stage parents or spouses."

"Do you . . . Is your mother . . . ?"

"No, uh-uh. My mother's long gone. She had a lot of problems, but not that one. I'm on the board of the Connecticut Alzheimer's Foundation. I go to a lot of luncheons—Alzheimer's, diabetes, mother-daughter things for Junior League, Hospital League, Hadassah—"

"Hadassah?"

"Absolutely. Jewish people are devoted to their parents. I've done some wonderful Moments for my Hadassah girls. You know how it is—they pass my name around, and I have all I can do to come up with a new concept for each of them."

Caroline blinked. "You mean at these luncheons, you—"

"Caroline, you're a real estate agent, aren't you? In Westchester? Rye?"

"Yes."

"And half your clients call you up because they know you from PTA or church or other volunteer organizations, right?"

"Yes, but—"

"And you don't go to the League luncheon and hand out cards, do you? But that's where the potential clients are, and when they need to sell their houses, they think of that nice girl with the warm smile and the classic clothes. Right?"

"Sure, I guess—"

"Well, there you are. This is a service business, just like yours."

Right. Except that your clients wind up with very small plots.

Margaret went on unperturbed. "Listen, speaking of service, I have great news for you. We are really zeroing in. Brian MacCloud has reserved the week of May twentieth to caddy for your father." When Caroline didn't respond she added sternly, "That's a real triumph, Caroline. You can't imagine what it means to preempt a week of this fellow's time. Quite a few of the gentry are among his regulars, just for example."

Caroline turned in her seat belt, trying to project an attitude of enthusiasm and gratitude. "No," she protested, "I'm very pleased, really."

Margaret seemed mollified. "And Ewen, darling old Ewen will be delighted to entertain your father for the evening of the twenty-eighth. I'm really excited about that. He insists on providing dinner—a brace of something, a special pudding for dessert, and then all that lovely whiskey and Ewen's wonderful stories. He's a mad golfer himself, of course; they'll sip away and tell each other lies . . . really, it makes me misty to think about it."

May 28. On the twenty-eighth day of May, Charlie Mayhew will be dead. Caroline sat up straighter in the car and looked out the window to see where they were. *I can't do this*, she was suddenly thinking. *I have to get out.*

They had pulled into Margaret's driveway. "And when I think of the horrible end he'll be spared," Margaret said. "Well, no need to dwell on that, is there? Caroline?"

"Oh, sorry. No," she said slowly, "there's not much of an alternative, is there? It's St. Andrews and old Ewen, or the hospital and three kinds of horrible deaths. No question of what he'd pick."

Margaret sat sympathetically still for twenty seconds or so, then got out of the car and stood waiting. *Come on, Strongheart*, Caroline told herself, and got out, too. She followed Margaret obediently around toward the office, but halfway down the path she stopped. "Say," she mused. "Maybe I ought to ask him."

"Oh, no, Caroline. I don't recommend your doing that. No, no. Come inside; we'll talk there."

There was an overwhelming peppermint scent in the office. Caroline sat down on the couch, in the same spot where she'd landed two days before. It felt familiar and unnerving: cold comfort, like finding your desk on the second day of school. She pulled nervously at a strand of hair behind her ear. Margaret, dressed today in finely tailored gray plaid slacks and a white linen blouse, lifted a pile of folders and what looked like mail off her desk chair and balanced it all on top of the papers already on her desk. She sat down and swiveled to face Caroline. "First of all, wouldn't it be a touch selfish? Asking him to make the decision, I mean? Nice for you, but what would it do to his enjoyment of the Moment? Honestly, wouldn't he much rather just go off to play this gorgeous course and have his bridge with Ducky Duchess and his smoky whiskey with Ewen, and think of nothing but the pleasures of the Moment?"

"But do I have the right—"

"Why don't you tell him that he has to stop drinking? Tell him it's going to kill him."

"He knows."

"Ah. But he drinks anyway?"

"Yes."

"Then who's making this choice, really? You or him?"

"Well, ultimately he is, but—"

"It seems to me he's decided already. The only choice you're making is whether he goes in pain or in pleasure."

"Did any of your clients ever tell the, uh—"

"Beneficiary. Yes, one did, against my advice. Since then, I must tell you frankly, we've made it pretty much a policy that if the client insists on letting the Beneficiary in on it, we'll have to decline the assignment. Unless of course the client *is* the Beneficiary. Then they'd hardly make things awkward, would they?"

"Oh. No, I guess not."

"In this one case, the Beneficiary was the mother. The people were Greeks, people of comparatively modest means. It was touching, really; two brothers and a sister had pooled their resources to give Mother a big, lavish party aboard the QE2. Two hundred guests for an overnight cruise, everything available for the guests at no charge—masseuse, hairdressers, facial and makeup people, pools, squash and tennis courts—and then of course a dinner dance with two bands, one ethnic and one for the younger crowd. Then Mother was to pass away in her stateroom, with a burial at sea."

"Good Lord."

"Yes. Rather majestic, really, like something out of the *Iliad*. However, one of the brothers got . . . concerned and decided to tell Mother the whole story and give her the choice. She was very gratified, actually, and quite willing to go, but unfortunately, she told eight or ten people about this wonderful thing her children were doing for her."

"Even the . . . ?"

"Even the final outcome. She bragged about it to all these relatives. We had to abort, of course, and I had to change my phone numbers and all. Well, but that's not the worst; unfortunately, the woman then had no choice but to live on in misery. And then of course there was the embarrassment of those eight or ten people she'd told, who believed ever afterward that she'd been making it all up."

"Poor thing."

"Yes. But look, Caroline, perhaps in your case it's best to let it go. A pleasant fantasy, but not for you. I think you'd better let me drop you back at your car."

"No, I—"

The door from the office to the rest of the house opened suddenly, and the peppermint smell intensified. A slender young woman stood in the doorway, holding a butcher's brown paper package out at arm's length. She was wearing a gauzy Indian skirt and a turquoise T-shirt, obviously without a bra. She had light brown hair worn in a long braid, a single dangly silver earring, and a ring on nearly every finger. "Carrion again tonight?" she demanded.

"Yes, Sarah, we have steak for dinner. What is that smell?"

"Dead castrated bull. You bought it."

"Not the steaks. It smells like a candy cane factory in here."

"Oh, the soap. It's Dr. Bronner's." She disappeared for a minute and came back holding up a medicinal-looking bottle in her other hand. "Biodegradable and nonpollutant. Great for everything—floors, pets, mouthwash, facials, birth control. I'm doing the floors out here. Or I was, until the doorbell rang and it was the deliveryperson with *this*. You want me to hang it on a hook till it gets real rank, or what?"

"Put it in the refrigerator, Sarah. Did you tip him?"

"Of course I tipped him. I offered him a backrub, too, because he looked really tight, but he just took the money. Sad, huh?"

She was gone.

"My housekeeper," Margaret said. "She's a Brown graduate. Vegetarian, obviously. She's actually very good, but she buys only holistic products. I have to do the food shopping myself, of course, or we'd starve."

"Floor soap for birth control?"

"Who knows. I don't have the strength to fight her over the soap and the toilet paper and things like that. She won't use anything with propellant, either." She sighed. "But look, let me drop you back at your car now."

"No. I want to go ahead with it. You're right—there's no alternative."

Margaret was silent for a moment. "You have to be very sure, Caroline. Better take a week or two, or a month. Think it over." She stood up.

Caroline saw St. Andrews and the Duchess glimmering away. "No!" she said desperately. "I don't need to think. I'm really sure. Really."

Margaret sat down slowly, scrutinizing her. Finally she said, "All right. Let's see what we have. Then you can decide for certain. I've got . . . damn, where is that thing? Somewhere here I have your father's Moment, all the bookings, itinerary, hosts and sponsors. I was quite pleased with it—ah, here it is."

Caroline reached out her hand and took it.

"You notice there's no mention of Nicklaus. That's turning out to be more complex than I'd hoped, but I'm still trying."

"Actually, it's a long time since Princeton. Maybe Dad would be intimidated by Nicklaus. Maybe instead just some nice local people who'd be willing to make room in a foursome . . ."

"Dead cinch. I mean, with the Duke and Duchess befriending him . . . They're tacky as can be, incidentally, and not real brilliant, but they're good fun. And I'll bet your father can beat the Duke at golf."

"It looks like a wonderful week." Caroline spoke with extra warmth; she still felt as though her resolve was being judged.

"Not cheap."

"No. I didn't expect that it would be." She looked up from the itinerary. "But . . . you've booked a return flight?"

"Of course. I always do. I mean, how would it look—"

"Oh. Right."

"But they'll refund the unused part of the ticket. They do. Or what people often do is apply the ticket price to the conveyance cost."

"Conveyance?"

"Well, that is, if the funeral's to be here. It's very expensive, bringing someone back . . ."

"In a box."

Margaret nodded, frowning a little at the baldness of the word.

"I was thinking," Caroline said cautiously. "Listening to that woman the other evening—"

"Woman? Oh, Libby? With Mom in the Hermès bag?"

"Uh-huh. You might think this is as weird as Libby."

"I doubt it."

"Well, I was thinking about Dad's, uh, remains. After he's . . ."

"Yes."

"And I thought of something. This is going to sound bizarre. Did you ever hear anything about burial in outer space? I remember reading somewhere that there's a company—"

"Wait." Margaret jumped up and pulled open the file cabinet. "Caroline, I love the concept. Would you believe it, I even happen to have the brochure somewhere. I sent away for it when the press releases first came out. I've been hoping that someone would have the vision . . . It's not the sort of thing you can, you know, *suggest* . . . " She was flipping through folders, frowning in concentration. "Let's see, space burial. President Reagan approved it, you know. He liked the idea—American bodies first in space, and at a profit . . . Where *is* it? I thought I had it under Space."

"Maybe you'd have it under Outer. Or Ashes."

"Maybe. Let's look. Abercrombie & Kent . . . AirRiders . . . Alnwick Castle . . . Artists . . . Ashes. Yes! Here it is! How did you know? I remember now—it was in the *Times:* 'Send Your Loved Ones into Space.' Ten thousand dollars a pound, but you can send just one pound if you want."

Sliding precipitously into hysteria, Caroline found herself wondering how much the average container of whole cremated person would weigh. Pulverized, of course. *What if I have some of Dad left over, after we fill up the capsule? Sprinkle the remaining remains over Cape Canaveral?* She focused sternly back on Margaret.

" . . . three different orbits, too," Margaret was enthusing. "Nineteen hundred miles up, or twenty-three hundred—that's the geo-synchronic orbit. But I think I remember reading that means you get stuck over a particular spot on the earth. I mean, it could be lovely, but—"

"Imagine spending eternity hovering over Secaucus."

"Exactly. But then there's the deluxe one, into deep space. How thrilling."

"I thought of it because my father's a space nut. He just

loved the moon walk. We watched it together. He stayed sober the whole day: not a sip. Doing his part as an American, he said."

"The only problem is, I don't think they've sent anyone up yet. So there's temporary storage of the ashes to contend with, until they begin their launchings."

"I thought about it, actually. I think I'd keep them . . . him . . . the . . . in the bar."

"Of course. And you know, you'd save money if you had the cremation there in Scotland. You could just have them ship the canister home."

"Ship it? Like a Christmas package?"

"We do it here all the time. Parcel post, UPS, whatever."

"Jet-propelled ashes. A sort of practice run, before he hits high torque."

Margaret shot her a look, two parts inquiry, one part disapproval.

"A joke," Caroline said.

Margaret smiled unconvincingly. "We'll have to arrange your day, too," she said.

"My day?"

"May twenty-eighth. Part of our service is to make sure that someone can vouch for your presence far away from the scene of the demise. It's for your safety, of course."

"My God. I never thought of that."

Another smile from Margaret, a serene, in-charge one. "Your father will be a continent away, but still it's best to be safe. There will be an inheritance?"

"Oh. Some, I suppose. Not enough to murder for. Not even enough to pay for this, uh, his Moment."

Margaret made a tiny, sympathetic noise.

"Don't worry. My ex-husband is paying for this. Or the settlement is. I can afford it. Anyway, what do you do on the twenty-eighth, assign me a shadow?"

"Nothing so dramatic. In fact, we like to keep this to the very, very ordinary. You could arrange it on your own if you wanted to, but we find that people are naturally apt to be a little edgy, and their friends—even their usual manicurists or tennis teachers or whatever—are likely to notice that and remember it. In the summertime we often arrange for a day of golf or sailing—"

"I don't sail."

Margaret blinked, reflecting the sudden hard tone in Caroline's voice, then passed over it. "Anyway, this will be a little early for sailing. Let me suggest a day at Elizabeth Arden, in the city. That's a very good one, because we can schedule it to go right through the afternoon, twelve to five, which is ten P.M. in Scotland. So obviously you could never get over there in time to be involved in the demise itself. And it's particularly good because the masseuse can even identify your birthmarks, if need be."

"Alibi day at Elizabeth Arden. My God. What time will it be, anyhow?"

"What?"

"The demise."

"I won't let you focus on that, Caroline. There's no need for you to know. *I* don't know, exactly. Let's think about making it wonderful. Shall we see what we have? Two round-trip flights to Dallas on April seventeenth, business class, and reservations at the Mansion on Turtle Creek in Dallas for four nights, two double rooms. Smoking or nonsmoking?"

"One of each. He smokes, too, of course."

"Okay. Two days to choose and fit the clubs, a day at leisure, one more half day to fit from the models. Next: he's reserved at Baltusrol for two weeks—there's only one hotel thereabouts that's any good, got him a deluxe room there, double, and I'll specify smoking. Then on May nineteenth, one first-class round-trip flight to Glasgow, changing over in London. Actually, I have another client going over on that very same flight, also flying alone. Dominick. This man is worth upward of sixty million dollars, and all he wants out of life is to have a week with his old war buddies, prowling London. His wife's arranging it for him. Dominick is a sketch. He called me up—thinks I'm the travel agent, which in a way I am—and declared that he always takes travel insurance in the name of someone who's recently done him a courtesy, and that he was going to name me as beneficiary on this trip, because I'd taken the trouble to research all his old haunts. Isn't that adorable? He'll forget, of course.

"Where were we? Oh, the flight. Is first class okay? We book all our overseas flights that way, except for some Jewish and Italian grandmothers. They tend to resist first class. I've had one turn around and trade her seat with some soul in coach. Okay, first class. Now: accommodations at the Old Course Golf and Country Club, got him a gorgeous room overlooking the seventeenth fairway. He can look right out and see everybody making fools of themselves. That's the killer hole, you know. Incidentally, they have a bar on the grounds and one on the top floor. Let's see: Brian MacCloud caddying for the week. Dinner and bridge at the Duke and Duchess's on the twenty-fourth. Dinner with Ewen on the twenty-eighth, all set. Now, let me add the space orbit. I'll have to research that, bring my information up to date."

She made some additional notes in silence, then looked up. "Now, what do you think, Caroline? Want to let it go for a month or so while you—"

"No. It sounds spectacular. I can just see him there at his window, checking out the seventeenth hole."

"Shall we cancel Dr. Gray's consultation? Make it simply a lovely vacation? Your dad is already booked for the return flight."

THE GRACEFUL EXIT

"No."

They looked steadily at each other for a moment. No one blinked.

"All right," Margaret said gently. "Will you want to fly over there on the twenty-ninth, then? Or shall I arrange for the technicalities to take place there, in your absence? You would have a service here, of course."

Arrange the technicalities. Bake at 1,000 degrees until undone. Transfer to suitable container and dump. Behave yourself, Caroline. "You arrange it," she said. "I don't know a soul in Scotland, and Dad didn't . . . doesn't . . . won't have known anyone either, really."

"Yes, much better this way. Oh, and speaking of Dad's knowing people, I've taken the liberty of arranging for videos of his stay in Scotland—on the course itself, action shots with Brian, at Braewick with the Duke and Duchess, and perhaps with Ewen? No? Certainly, I understand: not with Ewen. Incidentally, it's all done very discreetly; he'll never know he's being filmed. You'll be thrilled with the video. Now, what else? No returns, except for the unused airline ticket."

"What else would there be?"

"Well, quite often there's a major purchase—jewelry, say, or a baby grand piano or an airplane—and those things are all returnable, unless they're custom-made. It's one of the advantages of using our service. We have our arrangements made ahead of time, and we take care of all the details of the return."

"You mean you tell them when you buy it that this pipe organ will be returned, please pick it up next Wednesday? How do you explain?"

"When we make a purchase, I say that I represent a family who are buying this item for someone who's terminally ill."

Terminally ill as of next Wednesday at 3:45 P.M. Jesus. Caroline maintained impassivity. *Tell it to Janet,* she advised her-

43

self firmly. *Later. Right now, sit here and keep nodding. Or there goes Dad's Moment.*

"Normally they don't mind at all. They get a substantial service charge, and of course if there's any damage, the purchase is final. At any rate, your father's clubs will be custom-made, so I can't return them."

"I could donate them to Princeton's golf team."

"Super. A living memorial. What is it, Sarah?"

The housekeeper was back. "The lawn-service person is here. He wants to confer with you about spraying a substance on your trees that will cause mutations among the birds and insects and probably give us lung cancer at the same time. His name is Kevin and if you interrupt him in his transmission, he starts all over again from the beginning."

"Just tell him to go ahead and spray."

"I'm sorry, I can't do that. I won't be responsible for chemically induced mutations, especially since I don't believe that shrubbery has a greater intrinsic value than gypsy moths."

Margaret sighed, got up, and followed Sarah out of the office, raising her eyebrows at Caroline on the way. The pile of papers she'd balanced on her desktop slid slowly toward the edge and onto the floor. Caroline sat there a moment, then got up and began picking up the envelopes, file folders, and loose papers.

When Margaret returned, Caroline was sitting at the desk, a huge pile of folders on the floor, two smaller piles of papers on her lap, and a business envelope in her teeth. The desktop was clear except for a pile of unopened mail and the papers on her father's Moment. She blushed and took the envelope out of her mouth. "Sorry," she said. "There was an avalanche here, and I was trying to reorganize things a little so there'd be room for everything."

Margaret scanned the scene with a sharp eye, but all she said was, "I know. This desk is a disaster. When it gets impossible, I clean it all up and file things. You'd never know it, but I do kind of have a system."

"Oh, I hope I haven't destroyed it. It's just that everything started falling in all directions."

"No problem. That's how I know it's time to reorganize. I'll get to it this afternoon. Only right now I have to move the cars and show them where to stow the lawn furniture before they spray. It'll only take a minute. Do you mind? Then we can finish our paperwork and go for lunch."

As soon as Margaret left, Caroline resumed her sorting, stepping up her pace a bit; the idea of leaving a job half-done always made her a bit uneasy. Besides, there were things in these files that she wanted to have a look at. One of the good things about being a real estate agent was having the license to look around in people's houses. Every house was an open statement about its family—who had the power, what was important to them, what percentage of their lives was displayed and what hidden. You could see it all without seeming nosy. But this was even better—this was the orchestration of deaths. By whom? Whose deaths? Why? What was their idea of a good Moment? How much would they pay for it?

Most of these folders were like the ones Margaret had pulled out of her file cabinet—research materials on vacation spots, cultural events, items to purchase, sports trainers and the like. Those Caroline had already piled up on the floor. But some of them were files like the one on Charlie Mayhew, containing a brief profile of the Beneficiary, ideas for Moments, and rough outlines of the Moment itself as it emerged, all written on various sizes and colors of paper in a strong blue scrawl. The loose papers, which Caroline was now sorting, using the fingers of her left hand as dividers, had escaped from, or were not yet filed in, these Moment files. She'd already figured out that someone named Bussmeyer was going to take a trip around the world on the Concorde: London, the Bolshoi Ballet, Tutankhamen's Tomb, the Taj Mahal, the Great Wall of China, Hawaii, the Aztec Pyramids, and Barbados, all in twenty days. "Must be in a hurry," Caroline muttered. She was trying to decipher a notation scribbled on half a sheet of typing paper when she heard Margaret approaching. She released all the loose papers and buried them under a neat pile of Moments files. She was lifting other piles of documents onto the desk as Margaret came in through the garden door. "What if you had those bin things on your desk?" Caroline asked right away, to cover her guilty flush. "You could toss things into them by category—you know, mail, bills, research stuff, and so on. Also, did you ever think of using colored folders for the, uh, Beneficiary files? Like the one you have here on my father. If it were blue, say, you'd know that it wasn't your folder of Outer Space Burials."

"I'm hopeless. I'd probably end up with everything in the wrong color and it'd be even harder to find things. I'm an idea person—I get great ideas and reach for something to scribble them on, or pull out seven or eight files, and then there you are: chaos. Funny, my clothes are always in order; I mean, I hang things right up and put jewelry away."

Obviously, Caroline thought.

"Anyway, now that you've made order, let's make sure we've completed our plans for your father's Moment and then treat ourselves to a little lunch. I'll send you a copy of the contract next week to sign and return with a deposit."

Twenty minutes later, Caroline followed Margaret out of the office, which she would never have any reason to see again. She looked back once, thinking regretfully that she would never know who was in those other folders, or where Beneficiary Bussmeyer would drop out of the world tour. Barbados, maybe. Between piña coladas.

FIVE

"HI, DAD! HOW was your day?"

"Oh. Hiya, Pickles. Great, great."

"Really? Did you play?"

"Couple holes. Hey, you know? I think I'm finally correcting that slice. Maybe they gave me a transfusion from a scratch golfer. Whaddaya think?"

"Could be. Want to go back for another pint?"

"Nope. Who knows whose blood I'd get this time? Could be there's one guy in the world with a worse swing than mine. Anyhow, there's probably a club rule against improving your game any way except by paying the pro thirty bucks a minute to tell you how hopeless your grip is." His voice turned serious. "I'm not going back to the grimatorium, Caroline. Never. Not if they gave me a swing transplant from Palmer and a seventy-year lease."

"Okay, okay. Are you eating?"

"Sure. What about you? Sell that house?"

"Accepted offer. The engineer's going in tomorrow to inspect it."

"You're never going to meet anybody in that job, you

know. Except married guys with three kids and mortgage headaches."

"I know. Don't—"

"You don't need the money that bad. You love the job so much?"

"There are good things about it. We were talking about you. Meals, remember? You have to eat real meals and get your strength back, Dad. I'm planning a surprise for you; you have to be in shape for it."

"Hey, no surprises. You surprise a guy my age, you're liable to end up with a corpse." He chuckled. "Listen, at my age, a hole in one could thrill me to death. Although that's not the worst way to go, come to think of it."

"I'll be by tomorrow night—we'll have supper together. Get some sleep, okay?"

"Yup. Yessir. You get some fun."

"Okay."

■ ■ ■

"You never called me back."

"Why, so you could call me Little Mary Sunshine again?" Caroline wiggled out of her tennis shorts and unlaced her sneakers. She pulled her T-shirt over her head, then was stuck with it looped around the phone cord. She held the receiver away from her ear and disentangled it. Janet's voice came, nasal and inexorable, from the receiver.

"Some murder-for-hire broad who's pushing Valium on strangers can't find a file and right away you get that organizing gleam in your eye and that poor-thing-she's-got-it-tough tone in your voice. I've seen it all before, you know."

"Drop dead. Anyway, you should see what's in those files."

"I knew it; you cleaned up the whole thing, right? What's in them?"

"Never mind."

"All right, Caroline. I'm going to call the *Reporter Dispatch* and tell them everything I know."

"That won't take long. I'll hold on."

"I'll give you one more chance. What's in the files?"

"All I got to see was one on Bussmeyer, that's the Beneficiary—"

"Beneficiary. Does that mean he's the one who's sticking around?"

"Departing. Going around the world on the Concorde, in fact. Stopping off at the high spots. I figure he'll check out for good in Barbados. Maybe Hawaii, though. She has a vegetarian housekeeper who washes the floors with birth-control soap."

"You drinking?"

"You want to hear this or not? The only thing left is to put down thirty percent on my father's Moment—"

"His what?"

"Moment. Capital M. His ultimate golf experience; I'll tell you all about that. But the point is, we finished the planning and I left her office and now I'll never know what was in all those files. Janet, it's the most unbelievable thing. You sit in this lovely garden room and she books you into Elizabeth Arden for a day of beauty—you know, on *the* day—and some woman comes in with her mother's ashes in a Hermès bag—"

"Order Chinese. I'm coming over."

"Bring me back my gray Pringle. I'm seeing Simon this weekend."

"The wimp with the mustache?"

"Bring the sweater."

■ ■ ■

Before she could get into the shower, the phone rang again.

"Caroline?"

"Yes?"

"It's me. How are you?"

"Hello, Peter. Just fine, thank you. Did you have some reason for calling?"

"Come on, Callie. Can't we let that go? No reason we can't be civil. It's two years now. I called because I heard that your father was in the hospital. I always liked him, you know."

"I know. He's out, and he's feeling okay. Says his slice is improving."

"Hah! He'll say that till the day he dies."

"I imagine so."

"So he's okay? I thought maybe his liver—"

"A little angina. He's fine now. I'll tell him you called."

"Good, good. Hey, by the way, I have some good news, too. Thought I'd tell you before it got around . . ."

You waiting for me to ask what your good news is, Peter? Hold your breath.

"Kate's pregnant," he said finally, too heartily. "Seems we're going to have a baby. It's a boy—we had amniocentesis, you know, because—"

"Congratulations," Caroline said, unconsciously running a hand back and forth across her own flat stomach. "I hope he's just like you, Peter."

Later she felt sorry for saying that. What if you could curse a baby? *I didn't mean it, God. Only for a minute.*

Six

"PASS ME THE lo mein. So did you just hang up?"
"I don't know. No. He flapped around for a minute before he hung up—you know, take care of yourself, best to your father, that stuff. When did you get so good with chopsticks?"
"Diet."
"What?"
"It's a diet thing. If you only eat what you can pick up with chopsticks, you end up eating slower and—"
"I don't really hope she miscarries. I don't even know her. I just don't want Peter to have everything."
"You know what I want for Peter?" Janet smiled blandly.
"What?"
"I want him to hit forty and wake up impotent. Then I want her to cheat on him with a younger man and leave him flat. In all senses of the word."
"I don't wish that on him," Caroline said, alarmed.
"You probably don't," Janet said disgustedly. "Too damn bad. A little vengeance is great for the soul."
"It gives me a stomach ache. Anyhow, I have you for that. You are a very vicious and loyal person, Janet. Very vicious, and I want you to know that I appreciate it. You can keep

the Pringle until next weekend. I'll dazzle old Simon with anover—another—"

"Have another Tsing Tao. You're a generous drunk, but you know what? You can't spare the sweater; it's the only thing you own that shows you have boobs. Your wardrobe situation is pathetic. No, look—come in here—look at this—"

"You're dropping noodles. Get back here."

"C'mere. Look at this. Are you kidding? A little gray sweater-vest with Scotties on it? Five . . . no, six white blouses? Look at this skirt—it's so tweedy it doesn't need a person in it. The sexiest thing in this closet is that green silk blouse you wear at Christmas." She shook her head. "I'd kill to have a body like yours, and you wrap it in sacks by Abercrombie and Fitch. You know who you're going to dazzle with this stuff? Simon the Outstanding."

"I'm sick of Simon. I'm sick of my job. If I never see another center-hall Colonial, it's too soon. You know that? You have any idea how many disgusting basements there are in this town? Did you know that half of all buyers of houses in this community bring their mothers to see the house and Mommy doesn't like it and then we get to keep looking and see some more disgusting basements? Do you know that there are people who tell you for six months that they must have a modern house with a kitchen facing south, and then some other agent takes them out once and they fall in love with a Tudor with a northern exposure and buy it in a day? Tell you what let's do. Let's go buy me a whole lot of sexy clothes and then let's quit my job and I'll be something where you meet unmortgaged men and I'll meet a really wonderful—"

"You might just be tipsy enough to buy a decent outfit, anyway. Come on. Bloomie's is still open for an hour and a half. Let's roll."

"White. I want everything white. You know that's very glamorous? She always wears white. You know, and cream."
"Who, Vampira? I could have guessed. Get your shoes."

■ ■ ■

"You look great. Is that a new outfit?"
"This is its debut."
"I love it. It's really sensuous. I like the blue, too. You look very female tonight—how do you feel?"
"Terrific. Simon, I'm thinking of giving up real estate."
"Oh, I wouldn't do that."
"Why not?"
"Well, you're your own boss, so to speak; your time is flexible, and it seems to be a good living. Anyway, what else would you do?"
"I don't know. I'm not all that inept."
"No, of course not. I only meant it seemed to suit your needs."
"It did? What needs are those?"
"Well, I mean, a single woman living in the suburbs . . . you don't want to start commuting, do you? And it's something you can always do. I mean, no one's going to retire you—"
"Jesus."
"What?"
"I just had this image of myself at ninety-seven, tottering into my five-thousandth split level and saying, 'Marvelous use of space here.' I'll probably be selling the same houses three and four times over. A life in house-mongering, what a pleasant thought."
"Okay, okay. I'm sorry. Really. I shouldn't have butted in. You need to explore your potential."
"Explore my potential. It sounds as though you memorized that from the Single Male's Phrasebook."

"Are you premenstrual?"

"I'd better be. No, sorry, Simon. I'm sorry—don't pay me any attention. Where were we when I got so nasty?"

"Your needs. I was thinking of addressing them. I was thinking of paying you some pretty intense attention, as a matter of fact."

"Can you sleep over?"

"You bet. Got to be out by seven, though."

"Seven? In the morning? What for?"

"Told the kids I'd drop by and see their school photos before they left for their grandmother's, and they're leaving at nine, so—"

"Drop by? Ellen's place is an hour from here."

"Right. That's why I have to be out by seven. I mean, the kids think I'm sleeping at home, so to drop by Ellen's from there at eight or eight-thirty would be no big deal. Comprenez?"

"Uh-huh. I get it."

■ ■ ■

"Caroline?"

"Yes?"

"This is Margaret. From Greenwich?"

"Hi!"

"Listen, I've decided not to use the mails any longer for business correspondence. I sent something—it was to a friend, actually, a response to an invitation—and she never got it, and that made me stop and think about things getting lost in the mail."

"Oh. Of course."

"From now on, I'll have to finalize the paperwork, have it signed, and collect a deposit while the client's in the office, but here I am with yours and I wondered—could you possibly come by tomorrow and sign it?"

THE GRACEFUL EXIT

"Sure. That's fine. I have a morning appointment, but I ought to be done by ten-thirty."

"Anytime before noon is fine. After that I have a luncheon that will probably go on all afternoon. It shouldn't take us very long; nothing's changed since we spoke, just got some numbers finalized. I'll just ask you to sign the order for services and write a check? If you remember, we ask for thirty percent of the total."

"Sure. Fine."

"Caroline, you're an angel. You can find your way?"

"Yes, I'm sure I can."

In fact, she got out her county atlas and drew herself a little map and secreted it in her handbag. *I'm more excited now than I was all Saturday night with Simon*, she thought. *Caroline, you're getting strange.*

SEVEN

HER MORNING APPOINTMENT was a second visit to a huge Tudor, with the scent of a pending offer in the air. The client, a large young woman named Grant who had seen every house that had come on the market in the last four months, met Caroline out front. With her was a tall, attractive bearded man wearing jeans and a plaid shirt. "This is Charles," the client said. "He's a kitchen person." She smiled kittenishly at Charles, who flipped the smile back at her with camaraderie, dignity, respect, and the least hint of warmth. *He must practice that in front of a mirror,* Caroline thought.

Charles had an opinion on the heating system, the carpeting, the windows, the patio, and the flaking paint at the back of one of the closets. "Not a water problem," he pronounced. "They probably used latex over oil paint. No problem to fix it." It was ten o'clock when they got around to the kitchen. At eleven, Charles was measuring walls and checking upstairs and in the basement for plumbing lines and bearing walls, with Mrs. Grant trailing after him, chattering about the relative merits of the SubZero refrigerator. At eleven-thirty, Charles was sketching. It was ten minutes to twelve before they left the house. Caroline left, anyway; Mrs. Grant was still standing beside Charles's van, working the smile.

There was no time to stop and phone Margaret. She sped toward Greenwich, hoping to get there before Margaret left. She felt all the urgency of a movie chase scene. *Why are you so excited about making a down payment on Dad's untimely departure?* she demanded of herself. But it wasn't that; it was the prospect of getting back into that office. *Pathetic,* she told herself. *This is what you do for thrills?*

Sarah answered the doorbell. "She's gone," she told Caroline. "She asked me to tell you that she's very sorry, she couldn't wait any longer. Here's your folder, though; she said you'd know what to do. Sorry."

"No, it's my fault; I was very late. She had a luncheon, I know."

"The Connecticut Council on the Aging. It seems a little counterproductive to me, to sit around eating filet mignon while you discuss the problems of senile old people who'd probably be in great shape if they hadn't sat around eating filet mignon. The hormones in the beef alone could—"

"Go ahead and answer that."

"Oh, I don't ever answer this line. The machine will cut in after . . . there, see? After three or four rings. Listen, can you excuse me? I have a friend here, and I was just about to hypnotize him. He's trying to break his chemical dependency."

"Drugs?"

"Burger King."

"Go ahead. I'll let myself out. This may take me a little while."

"No problem. Just close the door real firmly when you leave."

She watched the girl depart, waited for a moment, then leaned gently on the hall door until it clicked solidly closed. The same confusion of files and papers covered Margaret's desk. She slid into the chair, opened the folder Margaret had left for her, and read slowly through the Outline of Services. It included a whopping charge for "Counseling," which she assumed was Dr. Death's fee. Carefully and deliberately she wrote the check to Great Events, Inc., and then noticed that there was also a separate sheet. It had only one cryptic line: "One pound capsule, Deep Space," it read. "$10,000."

One pound. Caroline closed her eyes. "I'm not ready," she said. "I'll deal with outer space later." She put the check and all the papers back in the folder. Then she sat down behind the desk and, keeping the folder on her lap in case she heard Sarah returning, she leafed through the papers, looking for Margaret's bold blue scrawl. Here was one. Beneficiary Paula Loadick. *"Age 49,"* Margaret's note read. *"Unmarried. No sports, no hobbies except church—sodality, retreats, etc. Teaches Spanish. Client is Paula's sister, Jacqueline Schlitz. Jackie requires that Paula depart before M's w.p., June 30."* M's w.p.? Somebody's wedding party? Caroline frowned and read on. *Paula's school ends June 20. Departure must be between June 20–30.*

"Not much time there for a Great Event," Caroline muttered. "Poor old Paula will hardly have a chance to brush the chalk off her skirts." She wiggled deeper into the desk chair. *"Possible:"* she read, *"arrange a miracle? Vision? Smoke machine, voice from the walls? Could get Hal Rowan to do voice. Special effects team from Astoria Studios. Use Jackie's summer house? (Edgartown—too far for Astoria team?)*

*"Possible: set up romance with ''priest''? Beneficiary loved Thorn Birds. Arrange retreat? No—a vacation. Mexico? Arizona? N.W. Pacific? Plant ''priest'' there. Long walks, poetry (Gerard Manley Hopkins). No sex—everything but. Look for: tall, solid

build, good voice. Take-charge guy, but sensitive. Talwell would be perfect—is he still on tour with repertory group?

"*Lodgings for romance*—should be spare but comfortable and private—"

A rap on the window startled Caroline so that she nearly knocked the papers off the desk. It was a woman, peering in through the window and looking surprised. Caroline had no choice; heart pounding, she went to the door and opened it. "May I help you?"

"Oh, no, I—it's just—is, uh, is Margaret there?"

It was Libby. No doubt about it—Caroline recognized the voice. She looked her over quickly: no Hermès tote bag. *What have you done with Mom?* she thought, but she smiled her reassuring-clients smile and said, "Margaret is out. I'm assisting her for a little while. Can I be of some help?"

"Oh, no, I just wanted to tell her something. Ask her advice, really. I can come back later . . ."

But as she spoke, she had edged into the office and was now standing in front of the couch, looking around.

"I'll be happy to give her a message," Caroline said hastily. "She'll be returning in the late afternoon, and I'm sure she'll get back to you."

Libby was leaning against the couch. She'd dropped her handbag onto the cushion. "I didn't know she had an assistant."

"Well, she sees all the clients herself, of course, but—"

The phone rang. Caroline started toward it, then froze. It rang again. She snatched it up. "Hello? This is Great Events."

"This is Jackie Miller, Margaret. About my sister, Paula? Listen, I was misinformed about the date when Mother's will probates." Caroline automatically grabbed a pad and began to take notes. "J. Miller," she wrote. "Mother's will probates." Holy cow, that was it: M's w.p.—Mother's will probates. Poor Paula had to depart before Mother's will probated. Or wait, didn't that Jackie have a different name? Schlitz?

"—*fourteenth*. Just one more little case of the lawyers working to Paula's advantage. This way she can start spending the money on her vacation. Or better yet, she could donate a series of stained-glass windows to that church of hers in Ma's memóry. Notre-Dame-on-the-Sound."

Miller or Schlitz, this Jackie was definitely the sister of the Spanish-teaching religious spinster. "That's June fourteenth? Two weeks earlier than we thought. Well, let's see. Does she get any time off in May?" Charged with adrenaline, Caroline was listening for Sarah, watching Libby edge over toward the desk, and trying to think of a way to do Paula in before school let out. She subtly blocked the desk with her body, backing Libby off with a territorial smile.

"They get a week off. Regents exams or something. But that isn't enough time—"

"Well, wait. She could meet him that week. Jackie, can you hold on for just a moment?" She put the call on hold, tore a piece of notepaper free and held the paper out to Libby. "If you'd like to leave your name and number, I'll let Margaret know you were here," she told her. "Or you can call late in the afternoon."

"Oh, that's okay. I can just wait."

The woman was about to settle into the couch. Caroline took a step forward and grasped her hand. "I'm sorry," she smiled. "Client's privacy. You understand."

"Oh, I'd never talk."

"No, of course, but we do have to ensure everyone's comfort. Those are Margaret's rules, you know. So nice to have met you." As she spoke, she'd maneuvered Libby toward the door. Now she shook her hand firmly and saw her out. She locked the door after her and sprinted back to the phone.

"Jackie? So sorry. A call from Florence. Now, about May. Why couldn't we arrange a special award? Teacher of the year, say, and the winner gets a week's trip to Taos. She could meet him there and they could pursue their friendship—maybe he'd even persuade her to call in sick for another few days."
"A priest would do that?"
"Crazed with love."
"Hah. Yeah."
"In fact, why wouldn't a week be enough?"
"Are you kidding? My sister? It would take her that long to catch on that he was a man."
"You haven't met this fellow. He's very good. It won't take him three days." She was improvising wildly. She could just see Tallfield or whatever his name was, sweeping pale, diffident Paula off her churchgoing feet, like Heathcliff or Robert Browning.
"Six days at the least," Jackie said sourly. "I'm telling you, she's a case."
"All right. Give me a day or two to work on this. We have another appointment . . . when?"
"You're going to call me."
"Of course. Well, don't worry, Jackie. We'll take care of it for you."
"*Before* the fourteenth."
"Absolutely."
Caroline hung up the phone. She snuck a look toward the window: no Libby. She walked over to the window and casually stood on tiptoe, peering down. Libby wasn't in the shrubbery, either. Then she tiptoed over to the door to the hallway, eased it open, and listened. She heard some tinkling music and a low voice murmuring: Sarah, exorcising her friend's addiction to all-beef Whoppers. Steadier now, she pulled the door closed again, locked it, and returned to the

desk. She felt a wide grin spread across her face. Got rid of Libby and arranged a Great Event. Not bad.

By force of habit, she began writing a memo for Margaret outlining her phone conversation with Jackie, as though Paula's demise was an agency she and Margaret shared, six percent commission on a three-bedroom raised ranch. Then she stopped writing, tore the paper up into tiny pieces and dropped the pieces into her handbag. "Better stay here and wait for her to come back," she told herself. "Only safe thing to do. Can't leave memos around in my handwriting. Can't say it all over the phone, either. Well, as long as I'm here . . ."

Halfway through the piles of paper on Margaret's desk, Caroline thought of Dr. Death. She could just walk into that other room and pick up the phone and have a chat with him. Maybe he'd think she was Margaret and talk to her for real. She could find out how he did it and whether it hurt, and where he lived and if he was married. "Sure you could," she told herself. "He kills people for a living but he's really a nice single guy and he'd love to know there was someone out there who knew more about him than he knew about her. He'd just let it go at that. Clever, Caroline. 'I'd like a cement overcoat, please. What colors does it come in?' "

Anyway, there was enough in this mess on Margaret's desk to keep her happy. How about Beneficiary Goodfellow, whose daughter-in-law was sending her one way through the Golden Door? Or Mr. and Mrs. Black? She was giving him a drop-dead vacation: a photo safari out of the Mount Kenya Safari Club, suite 33 with wet bar and mountain views. Biplane and pilot laid on, with jeep and driver and carry-boys to follow. Bwana Black was going to his eternal rest in the bush in his Willis & George cavalry twills, with his wife in brief attendance; she would fly into Nairobi for just long enough to plant him and shed a tear in the Trophy

THE GRACEFUL EXIT

Room. What she was doing on *the* day was attending a Parke-Bernet auction with her decorator. Perfect. Everyone would see her there, but if she arrived after the thing began, there'd be no need to get into a conversation with anyone, and who doesn't look tense at a Parke-Bernet auction? Ah, Margaret, you genius. Hey, what was this? Just a note on the outside of a Neiman Marcus envelope: *"weighs 300 pounds—poss. to go hang gliding?? Call Reid Briggs."* Hello, Reid? Just how much can you hang from one of those gliders?

She heard the key in the door too late: Margaret was there in the office, looking elegant and startled. Caroline jumped up, still clutching her father's folder. "Libby came," she blurted, "and then the phone rang—you know, while she was *here*—so I had to answer it, and I started a memo to you, but then I thought I'd better not write it down—"

"I'm so sorry—what a hectic time you've had." Margaret didn't sound sorry. She sounded annoyed. She looked at Caroline and at the papers on her desk, but all she said was, "What am I going to do with poor Libby? She's a menace." She sat down on the couch and began rummaging around in her purse. She was wearing a cream-colored silk jersey dress. Taupe belt and shoes. She looked like the cover of *Town & Country*. "Don't ever be old and poor, Caroline, that's all I can tell you. This luncheon was the worst. So depressing, you can't imagine. Aha, here it is." She leaned over and dropped a piece of paper onto the corner of the desk. It was evidently the program from the luncheon, and on its cover was the familiar scribble. "Some poor soul who came right up to me at the coat check and started hissing in my ear, can you imagine?" She glanced over, taking in her desk. "Oh, you saint, you've made *order*." It was a slightly chill inquiry.

"I'm sorry, it's just that this person called and I needed something to write on, and then—"

"Slow down. Tell me all about it. Libby barged in?"

63

Caroline sat back down behind the desk and outlined the sequence of events for Margaret. When she got to the part about what she'd been doing while she waited for Margaret to return, she used a real estate agent's technique: just as the floorboards begin to creak, you engage the prospective buyer in diverting conversation. "By the way," she said, "I'm surely no one to be telling you how to run your business, but do you worry at all about having your clients' names right on the folders? I mean, what if someone—"

"Look at the name on your father's folder."

It was still in Caroline's hand. She looked at the name for the first time. It said Charles Canaxe. "Canaxe?"

"You're perfectly right. The names on the folders are not the clients' real names; that would just be looking for trouble. So I change them a little. I use whatever associations I can dredge up. With your father, for example, I changed *May* to *Can*, and *hew* to *axe*. So Mayhew becomes Canaxe. See?"

And Miller becomes Schlitz. Aha!

"I do all the names that way, except in the account books. This is a service organization. I book trips and order furs, arrange parties and so on, and of course our clients have names and charge account numbers. But those records are in a safe place."

"Oh, good."

There was an awkward silence. Caroline was about to stand up when Margaret said, "I do thank you for dealing with Jackie. Actually, that's a terrific idea, about the teacher-of-the-year award. I love it. Think how happy it'll make poor Paula. Do you know, she's forty-nine years old and reasonably well off, and she has never bought herself a new piece of clothing? People give her gifts or hand-me-downs, or she finds things in the hospital thrift shop. The only luxury she's ever allowed herself, outside of gifts to the church, was to have her adenoids out. Jackie lives in terror that her friends

THE GRACEFUL EXIT

will run into Paula when she's wearing their castoffs. Poor soul. I really hope I can get Greg Talwell to spend that week with her. Jackie told you the plan for her Moment? He'd make a *great* priest: tall, kind of solidly built, really straight black hair that falls into his eyes—*won*derful eyes—long fingers, a voice like a hot toddy by the fire. It would be the best week of her life."

"And then Jackie gets the spoils."

Margaret looked at her. "We have to think of Paula, not Jackie," she chided softly, disappointed at Caroline's crassness. "Does she have this Moment—or does she have nothing at all? If we don't hire Gregory to fall desperately in love with her in the mountains, it will never, never happen, and what will she have? Long, dreadful years of wheezing and serving brewed Brim at church suppers and wearing her cousins' stained clothes." She shuddered. It was clearly the image of the stained hand-me-downs that got to her.

"She's not sick at all?"

"Who, Paula? Healthy as a horse. But I ask you, what kind of a life is it?"

Caroline nodded, assuming an expression of bland agreement to cover the voyeuristic thrill that was shooting through her veins. <u>Some of them aren't even sick,</u> she thought. *This woman isn't engaged in mercy killing: she's into pest removal. So we're not just talking about sick people and Alzheimer's and depressed relatives; this is hate and jealousy and envy and greed and vengeance. This is every last deadly sin, first-class, deluxe, and charge it, please.*

"I know I shouldn't get involved, Caroline, but I can't help it. I want Paula to have this Moment. I want it to be glorious and breathtaking . . ."

Oh, it will. Every last breath.

" . . . and to make up for all the lost years."

Now. "I was thinking," Caroline said cautiously, feeling

her way, willing herself not to blush. "You have so much to keep track of here. So many people to, uh, take care of. And you don't like organizing things, but you really need to. Then, too, you're out of the office so much—luncheons and meetings and interviewing clients—I mean, who answers the phone when you're not here? I bet people don't want to leave messages on the machine. And who deals with Libby? Who takes care of the last-minute stuff that has to be done *now*?"

"I know. I really should have a secretary. But then, here she'd be, and what would I do with her? And then there's security—"

"Maybe she'd be here only when you weren't. And about security . . . you could trust someone who'd been a client. I mean, how could someone like that possibly tell?"

"My clients have money—enough money so that they're not going to need to work as a secretary."

"So call her an assistant."

"Even so, who's going to want the job? Stuck away in a house in the suburbs, working at odd hours—"

"Someone who wants the adventure."

She said it so quietly that it silenced Margaret, who focused on her for the first time since she'd come in.

"The adventure. You?"

She'd lost the battle; the flush burned in her cheeks and ears and neck. "Why not? It beats peddling fake French Normandies with water in their basements."

Margaret was considering her, looking at her sharply. "Why *this* adventure?"

"The people. The stories. I mean, what brings people to this extreme? What could be more fascinating? You want to know the truth? I look at those files and I can't stand it; I want to read them all. Like why does the three-hundred-pound person want to go hang gliding? And who wants him dead?"

"Her."

"Her? No kidding! See, that's what I mean. That's great stuff. I've always been an eavesdropper. You know, in restaurants and on trains where someone's spilling secrets to someone else? I always listen—I mean *actively*. I'll move to hear better, if I can. My mother used to tell me, 'Curiosity killed the cat,' and I'd say, 'But satisfaction brought him back.' "

"Curiosity could be very dangerous for the cat, this time." Margaret was observing her closely, obviously surprised by her ardor.

"I know. I think I need the risk, too. Does that make me sound crazy? I'm really not weird, just stuck."

"Oh, I know. What is your personal life like, Caroline? You mentioned an ex-husband once."

"Peter the Not-so-great, that's what my friend calls him. He's gone. I'm single."

"Children?"

"No. Do you?"

Margaret blinked. "One daughter," she said, a beat late. "You seem to me to be the type to stay married. Make a commitment and keep it, that kind of thing."

"I am. He wasn't. Peter was—"

"Wait, hold on." Margaret was checking her watch. "I have a woman coming in for a consult any second."

"Coming here? What about her car in the driveway?"

"She's got a driver; he's dropping her off." She glanced through Caroline's folder, flicking past the signed contract and the check. She laid the folder down on the desk. "Do you want to stay?"

"Meet her, you mean?" Caroline's heart lurched.

"Try it out. It's that or hide in the laundry for an hour. You can be my assistant. No, wait; I'd better call you my partner. All right? Just a tryout. We'll have to talk later, and I'll have to give this some thought."

"Fine. I mean—"

"Save your story about Peter. We'll get to it later."

"Did you say a woman? There are two people out there."

"Must be the husband. Here we go: you wanted to see the world, chickadee."

The husband was small and natty. He had the unmistakable glow of a recent workout. He held himself tightly, walked lightly and swiftly. *Let's not mess with him,* Caroline thought. The wife, a blonde wearing a pale blue sweat suit with leather trim and several simple, heavy pieces of gold jewelry, looked at him before she spoke. "We're ready to finalize the plans," she said. "I told Jerry, and he thought your ideas for the production of Daddy's play and the gala sounded wonderful."

Jerry said nothing. His eyes glittered.

"Oh, and I remembered that I wanted to tell you to be sure and get it reviewed—you know, written up for an article in the papers, something nice for an obit in the alumni quarterly and the *Wall Street Journal*."

Neither the man nor the woman had noticed Caroline at all. She had slid into a listening posture, and now sat as still as she could. Suddenly the husband spoke. "This leaves us with your mother," he said to his wife. "Why don't we make a package deal? We could hang her needlepoints in the Guggenheim, get the *Times* to review them, and knock her off, too." He turned to Margaret. "You got a special price, two at a time?" He was smiling a little. A very little.

Margaret smiled, too. "You don't mean that," she began.

He ignored her and looked at his wife. "We didn't make any production like this for my parents," he said.

THE GRACEFUL EXIT

"We didn't have to. Your parents were lucky."

"A coronary and an embolism is lucky?"

"You know what I mean. It was quick and easy for both of them."

"For you, you mean. Never mind. Write it up," he told Margaret. "We'll take it. Did you get the cut-rate director?"

"He's not cut-rate, Jerry," the wife protested. "He's an academic. I told you."

"Same thing. The guy isn't making a living, is he?"

Margaret cut in. "Yes, Colin has reserved the time. He's really looking forward to working on the play, Arlene. It's going to be a spectacular evening."

Margaret and Arlene went into a huddle over details for the gala that would follow the performance, black tie at some embassy. Jerry reached for the phone and embraced it like a lover, curling his body around it and turning away from everyone in the room. Caroline heard him say, "Give me Barney," and then could make out only the low monotone of orders being given. She busied herself with the papers on the desk.

"And the passing itself will be . . . ?" Margaret asked finally. Jerry hung up the phone and turned back to the two women. He reached for his wallet.

"You mean how to do it?" Arlene asked. "I thought that you—"

"Not how, when. After the gala? There at the scene of his triumph?"

"Sure," Jerry put in. "Use the director as the hit man. It shouldn't be a total loss."

"No! Daddy has to have time to see the article in the newspaper and get the phone calls and—"

"All right," Margaret interrupted smoothly. "Say three days later, then? Before it all fades?"

"No. Not until after the weekend. We have theater tickets

we waited six months for. Make it Monday."

"Monday. Fine. Now, we'll have to take care of your day, Monday—and yours, Mr. Eagle."

"I'm in Atlanta all day Monday. Wall-to-wall meetings. What do you need me for?"

"I just want to be certain that you're not connected with the ... passing in any way."

"Oh, I'm connected all right. By several grand and a string around my balls. What about you?" he asked his wife. "Want to come out to Atlanta? They got stores there, too."

"No. I want to be unconscious. I want to be out. Actually, I was thinking of having a little cosmetic surgery. I really couldn't bear to be awake, knowing that Daddy ... so I thought maybe I'd get my thighs done. You know, liposuction? That way I'd be anesthetized, and by the time I wake up ... "

"How about a sex-drive implant?"

"Funny, Jerry. I'm going to have my thighs done. I made up my mind. And I'll take Mother with me so she won't be, uh, connected with the passing, either."

"How are they going to get to your thighs when you and your mother are joined at the hip?"

"Jerry."

"Okay. But you better plan on forgetting about your birthday, then. This is it. After this you've had it for the year."

"Nice couple," Caroline said when they'd left.

"I told you, I see everything. Still think it's for you?"

"Are you kidding? This is the most exciting thing I can imagine. That man was a *thug*."

"Just a boor, I'm afraid. Actually he manufactures bathrobes." She was looking steadily at Caroline. "You were going to tell me about your marriage. Unless you'd rather not."

"No, no. I understand perfectly. You have to know about

me. Anyway, it's no secret. Everybody knew what happened four minutes after I did. Or four months before, more likely." She took a long breath. "He's famous, Peter, a famous litigator. You've probably seen him on TV. I married him because he was . . . he could make things happen. And he believed in himself completely. Peter was the most solid and powerful person I ever knew. He had all this *energy*."

"Different from your father."

"Exactly. But on the other hand, he *was* different from my father. Know what I mean? Not easy, not funny, except with sharp remarks. Never casual." She sighed. "He never passed out in public, though, and he wasn't late for everything, either. I'll give him that. Anyhow, he bought this boat."

"Sailboat?"

"Uh-huh. Thirty-five-foot Dufour. I hated that boat. I get seasick, so I was taking Dramamine all the time and then I'd be drowsy and clumsy. I could never get the jib down fast enough. But I *wanted* to do it, I mean I wanted to be a perfect sailor and a perfect boat hostess and . . . well, so when the boat was new he invited these people out for a day sail, another lawyer and his wife—Fenton and Mimsy Somebody. Mimsy had grown up at the Fisher Island Yacht Club. Teethed on halyards, probably. So she had the wheel and she didn't even have to think about it, you know? And when we heeled over she laughed and turned the damned wheel so we heeled some more. And Peter said, 'Let's not scare Caroline. I'm trying to convince her that this is not the Titanic,' and everybody laughed kindly."

"God."

"Right. Anyway, I'd made this lovely picnic lunch and I went below to get it ready to serve, and they suddenly came about and the cold watercress soup and the salmon mousse hit the walls and the ceiling, and it was all dripping down the cute little Dufour curtains—"

"Oh my God."

"Right, I shrieked, of course, and they ran downstairs—*below*—and when they saw the scene, they laughed like crazy. They thought it was a scream, that anybody would serve cold watercress soup and salmon mousse on a sailboat in the Sound."

"You poor thing."

"That Monday I went out and started studying for my real estate license. So on weekends after that, I was often showing houses and I didn't go sailing with him much. He had his sailing friends."

"And one day he sued for divorce and sailed off into the sunset with one of them. A twenty-five-year-old with braids and perfect legs, right?"

"Close. A thirty-year-old associate in his firm. Masses of drip-dry curly hair and perfect legs. I hear she's a wonder with the jib."

"She probably screws him in the riggings, too. They're all subhuman."

Caroline, who had been playing with the sash of her wrap-around skirt, looked up, jolted by the change in Margaret's voice. She sounded almost coarse. Her face, though, was serene and composed as ever. "Lawyers," Caroline agreed.

"Not lawyers, men."

"No, just lawyers."

"You still believe that? You're in a bad way. Listen to me, Caroline: they are all subhuman. Every last one of them, each in his own way. Amazing, the variety, when you think of it."

"But you're married."

"What's that got to do with anything? Everybody's married—except you, and you know why?"

"Because I got seasick."

THE GRACEFUL EXIT

"Not because you got seasick. That may be why your husband left you—that and the cutie with the perfect legs and the screwing in the rigging. But why you're not married *now*, to somebody else, is because you're a dreamer. You live in never-never land. You believe that there's a sensitive and true human male out there who was made for you, and you're hanging around waiting for him. If you knew better you'd be remarried by now to a suitable subhuman, like everybody else."

"Did you stay married or remarry?" Caroline felt entitled to ask: she'd spilled her story, hadn't she? Still, she looked quickly at Margaret's face to see whether the question had displeased her. Margaret smiled faintly and shrugged one elegant shoulder. "Stayed married."

"What does he think about your business?"

"Oh, Mac doesn't know about my business. He thinks I'm in corporate party planning. As long as I don't bother his business associates—and of course I don't; I never deal with anyone remotely connected with him—he doesn't care what I'm doing. Except that he likes to take off for a long weekend on the spur of the moment now and then, and these days I usually can't take the time."

"You could if you had an assistant."

"Mm."

"Look, I understand how careful you have to be. You can certainly check me out if—"

"I'm checking you out now. And of course I had you . . . looked into before our first meeting. I do that with every potential client before I ever meet anyone. I have to protect myself. There are lunatics out there. And deadbeats, and criminals."

"And cops."

Margaret raised her eyebrows.

"Not that—I mean, I know: you're simply a service, you just plan events and Dr. Gray is optional. Separate. But even so, it could be awkward . . ."

Margaret watched interestedly as she floundered. Finally she put up a hand to stop the rush of words. "You're right, it would be annoying. And a waste of my time and resources."

"That's what I meant."

"So I do a little homework in advance, and you checked out excellently. You're solid and loyal and discreet. Good business reputation, excellent credit, no psychiatric or criminal history, no questionable friends. No love life to speak of. Incidentally, I must tell you, you're not likely to find one here. There's absolutely no fraternizing with the clientele, of course."

Caroline's chest pounded and her lips went numb. "No, of course, I know."

"If you meet a client at a social event—"

"I play dumb. Never met him in my life."

"Exactly." There was a long pause. Caroline didn't stir. "All right," Margaret said finally. "Say, three afternoons a week, beginning a week from Monday?"

"A week from Monday."

■ ■ ■

"Mrs. Samson? This is Caroline Mayhew. I was in last week and I looked at a Perry Ellis skirt and sweater? It was off-white and the . . . Oh, you do? That's terrific. What a memory you have! Is it still . . . an eight . . . You do? Great! Can you hold it? I'd like to pick it up tonight. No. Well, yes, it *is* kind of a gift. From me to me. A sort of celebration."

EIGHT

"I'M THIRTY-TWO. They don't *do* the sex-change operation much past thirty-five or so. I mean, what would be the point? I've put it off all these years because Mom would die, you know? She would just pass right over. But I can't put it off anymore."

The man's voice was overmodulated. He was slender, but his face was slightly rounded, and he had plump, hairless hands with immaculate nails. He was wearing a nondescript gray suit and black loafers. He looked like a banker, or a small-town jeweler. Caroline tried to picture him as a woman. *Red wool dress with a turtleneck to cover the Adam's apple*, she thought. *Red-and-black enamel clip-on earrings.*

"I have a right to a life, too," he was saying plaintively.

"Of course," Margaret soothed.

"Do you know, they won't even start you on the hormones until you commit to the operation? Can I tell you how tired you get of *shaving* everything and binding that damn thing down out of the way? It isn't a normal life."

"No, it must be very wearing."

"Can't you just wax your legs and arms?" Caroline asked.

She felt her face flush. *Jesus, Caroline, don't be helpful. Just shut up, for once in your life.*

"Sure, but some things you can't wax. You want to talk about pain? So I wax, I shave, I tweeze. You can't imagine. Eleven years now. And can I just tell you? The men you get are weird. I mean, what kind of man wants a man who looks like a girl? Either you want a man or you want a woman, right? I want a man who wants a woman, plain old garden variety, no kinks. I am sick to death of kinks."

"And what about Mother?" Margaret inquired. "Is she ill?"

"Sick, very sick, but not ill, if you know what I mean. Four hundred years on the couch wouldn't make a dent, but the woman is an ox, an absolute ox. Never gets a cold, even. Never breaks a *nail*. If I wait for her to croak, I won't have any sex left to change. I'll be one of those tottering old neuters."

"I understand. And if you go ahead with the operation now, you want to spare your mother the shock."

"Exactly. You understand exactly. You're a very sensitive person."

"Thank you, Lowell."

"Laura. That's my real name."

Not a blink or a swallow; Margaret was amazing. She wrote it down on her pad and went right on. "Laura, do you have an idea what kind of peak event you want for Mother?"

"Pavarotti. All she wants in this life is to meet Pavarotti. I'll tell you the truth, I think what she'd really like is to go to bed with him. And wait till you see her—the whole person is five foot one, a hundred and three pounds, *counting* the hairspray and the uplift bra. I figure all he'd have to do is roll over in his sleep; that alone would do her in, am I right? But of course it would be a scandal and a mess for him the next day. Anyway, why on earth would Pavarotti want to—"

"Oh, Laura, I hate to tell you but you've hit on the holy grail. Totally unavailable. Everybody wants Pavarotti—*everybody*—but it can't be done. It's the one kind of appearance he will not do."

"Well, I mean I didn't expect that he'd go to *bed* with her. Just dinner would be okay. Lunch, actually, one of those endless European lunches with—"

"Not even a diet Coke. Believe me, I've tried. What about . . . let's see, if she likes twinkly and cuddly I could try for dinner with Herschel Bernardi."

"Herschel Bernardi? I have an *uncle* the spit and image of Herschel Bernardi. The point about Pavarotti is that he's cuddly and twinkly but also exotic and foreign and sexy. And young—younger than her, anyway."

Caroline took a breath. "I have a thought," she ventured.

"Don't tell me Plácido Domingo. She can't stand how he did that album with—"

"I was thinking of Itzhak Perlman. For dinner, I mean, not for . . . well, just for dinner. I thought of him because when I was going through our files of celebrities and charities I saw his name, and he's apparently very charitable. He has this one pet cause. . . . I thought maybe for a huge contribution—"

"He's the one on the crutches? She *loves* him. She's always saying, 'Look at the expression. Look at the passion the man has—' "

"Fantastic," Margaret broke in. "Caroline, what an idea! I know just who to call at Carnegie." She tapped one nail on her desk. "What about a private seat at a closed rehearsal and then a tête-à-tête dinner afterward, say, on a Wednesday. He could tell her all about the music and what he's thinking as he plays—and then on the actual night of the performance, she could take a box with a few friends. Of course I have no idea whether he'd agree to it. Certainly it would have to be a very considerable contribution—"

"Oh my God, Sylvia Herman will sit there and die of envy. And Aunt Barbara, that's my aunt that Mom has loathed for thirty-five years. And that Carlotta woman with the son who's married to an investment banker and has two kids and an au pair . . . how many people can sit in a box? My mother is going to be delirious."

"Of course she could take any number of boxes. We could also do a private dinner for her friends at the Russian Tea Room before the concert. It's hokey, but for older people—"

"Delirious. 'At one point in our quiet little talk last evening,' she'll tell them, 'Itzhak told me and don't tell anyone I told you, it was really a confidence . . .' The woman will be out of her mind. She'd *volunteer* to die for this. I'm starting the hormones tomorrow."

■ ■ ■

Margaret put her hand over the phone. "Give me strength," she muttered. It was pouring outside, and the windows in the office had fogged up. Caroline was sitting on the floor, surrounded by piles of paper. Margaret spoke into the phone again. "Well, if Tyler has Parkinson's, dear, I wonder how safe he'd be, motor racing. . . . Yes, that's true enough, but he could injure others as well, and we want the Moment to be unflawed, isn't that right? . . . Yes, I see. Early stages. . . . Uh-huh, if he doesn't do it now, when will he? Isn't that the truth. Let me think, Ginny. It needn't be an actual race, just the experience, right? . . . Yes, the thrill of the raceway, I know. Say, how about a motor-racing school? There's that place Paul Newman went to—oh, thank you,

THE GRACEFUL EXIT

Caroline, that's just what I was looking for. Bondurant's, that's it. Nice location—it's in Sonoma, not far from the Silverado Inn and Club. Uh-oh, hold on, not so good: it says here that Bondurant's holds its clients liable for any damage they might do to the cars, and with Tyler having Parkinson's, you never know. . . . Yes, and besides being expensive, that policy is a touch punitive, don't you think? This is supposed to be *fun*. What? Oh, my assistant is showing me . . . ah, yes. Here's one in Salinas, the Jim Russell British School of Motor Racing—no, wait, it's just the central office that's in Salinas. He can take the course at Mont Tremblant, or how about Laguna Seca? That's not far from Carmel and Monterey. I could book him into Quail Lodge. That's a charming spot. Lovely suites, too. . . . Oh, will you? Separate rooms, I know. No, of course you should. What a thrill for you, to be there and to see him so happy. Well, listen to this, here's what they teach: double-clutching, heel-toeing into a corner, skid control—small classes, formula Mazdas—and no student liability for the cars. A three-day course, and you can also get a racing postgrad. . . . Yes? Now, let me check into their requirements before you get too excited. Well, medical exams, that sort of thing. You know, Ginny, if this doesn't work out we can always go to private lessons. . . . Well, then we'd just rent the raceway for the day and guarantee the car to the leasing company. All right, dear, I'll get back to you. Bye."

She turned to Caroline. "Can you believe it? Well, at least he won't have to worry about his car insurance rates going up afterward."

"Separate rooms? Is this the wife?"

"God, no. This is his cousin, Ginny Talner. I've known her forever. I've got her tagged in as Shortley on the paperwork, just so you'll know. She's been sweet on him since they were teenagers, and he's an absolute bozo. Incidentally, where'd you get that information from? I don't remember the stuff about the Jim Russell racing school."

"One of Peter's old sports magazines. I clipped the article and brought it in."

"Fantastic."

"It's in a new file, under Sports. R for racing."

"Uh-huh. You keep track of it, okay?"

■ ■ ■

"The guy has Parkinson's and he's bowing out in a racing car? In the driver's seat?" Janet raised her eyebrows. "Remind me not to be standing around in Monterey that day."

"Laguna Seca. Anyway, it probably won't happen while he's driving, although that would be nice for him."

"Nice for him. You sound like my mother. You know what they talk about in her condo? They sit around the pool and rank people's deaths. They say, 'That was a good death.' Or, 'Tch—a bad death.' They have, like, a scorecard. 'How'd old Freddie do?' 'Oh, he had a rotten death. Take five points off his total.' "

"Well, there *are* bad deaths."

"I know, and you and The Lady in White are doing great work. Actually, I'm looking for a gown for your Nobel award dinner. Is sequins too upbeat? What'd they wear to Mother Teresa's?"

"Shut up. And stop waving your fork around—you're going to get salad dressing on everything. Anyway, what about my father?"

"Since you started wearing all that beige—"

"Cream."

"Since you started wearing all that cream, a meal with you is like sitting at the housemother's table. I liked it better when you wore wall-to-wall tweed."

"What about my father?"

THE GRACEFUL EXIT

"What about him? That's different and you know it. Hey, it was me who sent you to The Lady in White in the first place, remember? You're doing the right thing. By the way, how's it going? He's all excited about the Duke and the trip and everything, right?"

"He's kept it to two drinks a day for the last week. I hope it holds. You know what he said? He said he felt like he'd won at 'Strike It Rich,' and where was his mink coat and his refrigerator-freezer? He's really thrilled. But I keep thinking, if he could just go on like this, hold himself to two drinks a day—"

"Can he, Caroline? Did he ever? This is a heroic effort he's making because he has something fantastic coming up in a week or two. Anyhow, you know what the doctor said. Cold turkey, cold sober, all day every day, forever."

"I know. He could never."

"So when does it start?"

"We leave for Texas on the seventeenth."

"Buy yourself a beige . . . buy yourself a *cream* knit with a little cleavage. You never know who you could meet in Texas. And silk pants; let 'em know you have an ass. Texans appreciate hindquarters. I'm thinking of moving there."

"I'll help you pack."

NINE

"OH, YOU CAN bet on it. What Trisha wants done gets done. That's because I don't go around wishing for things: I arrange for them to happen."

The voice carried through the open window, unmuted and self-satisfied. Looking up, Caroline saw Margaret walking rather quickly along the back path but failing to hurry her companion, a very thin, very elaborately dressed blonde. The woman wore a tight, short skirt; a sweater that seemed to have feathers and beads woven into it; a short, fitted jacket; and very high heels. Her hair, long, curly, and wild, was held on one side by a large barrette. She sauntered after Margaret, still talking at full volume, looking around at the grounds and the surroundings like a potential buyer, and finally allowing Margaret to shepherd her into the house.

She looked around appraisingly. "This is the office?" she asked. "Nice room. Who's your decorator?"

"I'll give you his name later, if you like," Margaret answered, clearly relieved to have gotten her charge indoors. "He's so busy though—people wait for months."

"Well, scratch that. Unless he wants his work featured in *Better Homes and Caskets*. Who's this?"

"This is Caroline, my partner. Caroline, Trisha Carr."
"Miss Carr."
"Hiya. All right, so this is the deal. We can talk now?"
"Absolutely. Please have a seat."
Trisha sat carelessly on the sofa, automatically flicking her jacket open and arranging her body in a provocative position. *She does that without thinking, even when she's alone,* Caroline thought enviously. *So she's probably never alone for long.* She pulled in her stomach and curved her back a little in imitation, easing her bust forward, but it felt silly, so she leaned back in her chair.

"I want you to arrange it so I die at home," Trisha said flatly. Caroline blinked. She had been looking Trisha Carr over pretty closely; this was no sick woman. Her eyes were bright; she moved with the ease of a runway model—it was obvious that nothing hurt—and she had an aura of crass, amused authority. People came into this office trying to hide their feelings, but Caroline read them all like neon signs: Anger. Depression. Fear. Bitterness. Guilt. Glee. Trisha Carr was hiding nothing; she was high, excited, delighted with herself. *She wants to fake her death,* Caroline decided, relieved. *This is going to be fun.*

"Wait till you see my bedroom, speaking of decorators," Trisha went on, perhaps unaware of Caroline's greedy curiosity and the alarm Margaret was clearly feeling. "It's fabulous. I did it all in pale, pale, pale pinky peach. Trapunto fabric on the walls, gauzy curtains, Berber carpet—vegetable dyed, by hand—chaise and bed upholstered in palest peach linen. Gorgeous. Anyway, that's the spot. In bed, doing it. In the act. Champagne, Montenapoleone nightgown, the works."

"Let me understand," Margaret said slowly. "You want to die now?"

"The second Friday in June. I'll just be back from Maui,

so I'll be tan; I'll look fabulous against all that peach. I already have my appointments for that week—hair coloring, leg waxing, pedicure, and everything."

Margaret shot a panicky look at Caroline: *Is she psychotic, or what?* Caroline raised one shoulder and one eyebrow in an almost invisible shrug: *Beats me.* She tried out her theory. "Really die?" she asked Trisha. "Or stage a death?"

Trisha blinked elaborately, a sign of impatience with a stupid salesgirl. "That's what you do, right?" she demanded. "Real honest-to-Christ deaths? I want one. The second Friday in June."

"I think Caroline asked the question because you look so fabulous," Margaret put in quickly. "And you seem . . . well, you don't seem upset."

Trisha nodded, accepting her due. "That's what I *said*. I want it now *because* I look fabulous. And quickly, because there isn't much time. It's going pretty fast now."

"You're ill?" Margaret asked carefully. Caroline, reluctantly abandoning her notion of a staged demise, switched to awed pity. This must be one of those incredibly brave, terminally ill people you read about, who go glowing and cheerful to their deaths.

"Not ill. Just going fast."

"Going . . . ?"

Trisha stood up and wriggled her skirt up to her waist. She had on silken little leopard-print panties. "See this?" She clutched her belly. She could pinch an inch. She whacked her thigh. It jiggled a little. "Disgusting. And look at this, look at my hand." The skirt settled onto her hips. "That's old skin. I'm *going*, it's all going down the tubes and I'm not sticking around for any man to do me a favor." She yanked the skirt down into place and sank back down into the couch, crossing her legs. "I'm not getting any older than this. You ever see a naked old lady? We went to the Dead Sea. You been there? No, I guess not. Well, there's a bathhouse there, and everyone undresses in this one big room. Bodies." She shuddered. "My God. Bellies like pouches hanging out, boobs . . . and you know those draped silk cowl dresses?" She described a long U with her hand, four fingers outstretched to represent the folds of the fabric. "That's how the skin on their thighs looked. I'd rather die. I mean literally, I would rather die, so that's what I'm doing. I told you, I don't wish; I arrange. I'd do it all myself, except I can't have it looking like a suicide. He's not going to have a chance to think that I killed myself over him."

Caroline leaned forward.

"As a matter of fact, I am going to get the son of a bitch with this one," Trisha said with satisfaction. "As long as he lives he'll never forget this scene. He'll never get it up again."

"Your husband?" Margaret asked.

"*Not* my husband. Although that would be a side benefit. Wake the schmuck up for once. He's usually the one who dies in bed. Beat him at his own game. But Leon—that's my husband—he's got nothing to do with this."

"Who is your target, may I ask? I might be able to help you enhance the pleasure if I know what we're after."

"We're after my lover. My ex. Jimmy. He dumped me for Suzanne Coates. *Suzanne Coates*—I mean, she works out in my health club, so I know what she looks like. She has no *tits*. And very superior. She never talks to anybody, you know the type? Actually, my first idea was to destroy her. I thought about sending a vibrator to her husband with a little note, saying, 'Maybe if you used this on your wife, she would stay home more. Ask her what she's been doing Monday and Thursday afternoons.' But I decided I like this better. Forget her; I'm going to fix old James so he never fools around again, with anybody.

"Get this." She sat up straight, recrossing her legs, and

flung her hair back. She smiled smugly. "A film: I'm in bed with this hunk, my new lover. We're making love—especially in this one position that Jimmy thinks he invented. There's a champagne bottle open on the night table, two glasses sitting there. Everything's in, like, a soft, rosy light. You'll have to arrange that. And I'm whispering to this guy—I'm telling him how Jimmy couldn't get it up half the time, and how I was always faking it with him. I say to him, 'You know Jimmy Diecker?' and he says, 'Yeah, I heard the name. He's in land development?' and I say, 'That's him. He's all the time erecting buildings. I hope they stand up better than his cock.' Then we both laugh, the hunk and me, screwing away and having a good laugh at old Jimmy."

"Will your lover actually laugh?"

"Jesus, do I have to do all this for you? You running a service here, or what? This is a setup. You get an actor to play the hunk, I'll write the script. That's your big job, to get the actor—I want a sensational body and I want a great voice. I mean, it should *sound* like he has a mustache and a great body and a three-foot cock. And you get it on film."

Caroline sat perfectly still, just sliding a glance toward Margaret. *She won't actually throw her out,* she decided. *She'll just say something friendly and regretful and absolutely final.* Margaret declining to produce a sex movie: this was going to be something to see.

"Videotape?" Margaret asked. She was making notes. Caroline blinked.

"Yeah," Trisha said. "Videotape, but it has to be one sensational photographer. First of all, no shots of the guy's face. Every guy Jimmy meets in the business from now on, I want him to be wondering: Is this the one? Is this guy laughing at me because Trisha told him I can't make it in bed?" She was smiling entirely to herself. "This is about humiliation," she added.

"I understand."

"Good. And second, no flab."

"I don't—"

"You ever see those porno flicks? If you have the least bit of flab, sooner or later it ends up hanging out, right on the big screen. I don't care how long it takes to film the thing, I don't care what you have to pay for editing: no flab. You got it?"

"Absolutely."

"And you make sure that Jimmy sees that tape. I need a guarantee. Otherwise there's no deal."

"We would never let you down. A last wish—"

"I'll tell you one more time: I don't wish. I arrange. I see to things. That's how I get my wishes."

"Jimmy will see the tape. We'll guarantee that."

"You figure out how and why. No anonymous mails, either. It has to be, like, official. First of all, if he figures out that I did it for revenge I might as well not have bothered."

"Right."

"And two—I told you, this is about humiliation. I don't want him to get away with seeing this thing in private. People know he dumped me for the titless wonder? Let him get a little taste of how it feels. I want a couple of guys—dressed like investigators or cops or something—I want them to bring him the tape, like it's part of an investigation, and I want them standing there and watching him watching the tape. Two big macho guys, hearing all about how Jimmy couldn't get it up." She smiled broadly. "After that, old James might as well hang it up and retire the number. I know him."

"We'll take care of it. Should this take place in his apartment or in an official setting?"

"At his place. Now here's the one question I have: how do you look when you die? I have to look sensational."

"One of the things we're very proud of is that our Beneficiaries look perfect. Perfect. No discoloration, no . . . odd expressions. Juliet on her bier, that's the effect."

"You have any pictures I could see?"

"No, I'm afraid not. We won't have yours, either. We guarantee absolute discretion; that's the whole point. Total anonymity. I promise you, though, it will be magnificent. Our photographer is—"

"He'd better be. I'll know, as soon as he starts shooting. Anyway, I'll tell him what I want. All right. Now, I've got a list. One, a cleaning service. My girl isn't worth diddly as a cleaner. Get the best; I don't want some smartass girl reporter finding dust under the bed."

"We have—"

"Two. Satin sheets. Pale peach. My decorator had mine made up for me, but they're cotton, and I think satin will show up better on the video. I'll give you a pillowcase so you can match the color."

"Scalloped or plain?"

"Plain. I go for simple and elegant, all the way. Three, an ice bucket. Mine is dented and I'm not buying a new one."

"The sheets, of course, will have to be an outright purchase, but I can find a lovely crystal ice bucket for you. Or we can borrow an antique silver one for you, from the collection of—"

"Great. But someone else will have to return it."

"We make those arrangements, of course."

"Right. Ice bucket is three . . . oh, four—on the stereo there'll be a record of Charles Aznavour. I'll tell you exactly which cut. He'll never hump to that one again."

"We'll bring a copy of the album to the taping. Also, we can dub it in as background, after the film is edited. Incidentally, we can go on location if that appeals to you. We don't have to confine ourselves to your home; we can go anywhere you like, a place where you and Jimmy used to meet, for example—"

Trisha grinned. "The old D.V. We never met there. It's the one place in lower Connecticut where we didn't make it."

Margaret waited. Caroline had been lost in a reverie for some time now, imagining Margaret engaged in negotiations to procure a stud for Trisha's home movie. She tuned back in on the conversation as Trisha said, "The *Double Vision*. That's our boat. Fifty-five-foot Gulfstar. Three staterooms and two full baths."

Heads, Caroline thought automatically. *Don't say baths, say heads.*

"The master stateroom has a walk-in cedar closet and a bathtub. Jimmy was dying to get it on there."

"What does the name mean?"

"Double Vision? It's from our business. We have an optics company. Lenses. You know the new tinted ones, turn your brown eyes blue? We have half the mid-Atlantic region sewed up. Leon thought up the name. He tells everybody the boat is our dream—double vision, lenses, dream for two, get it? He's so full of it. My dream. All I ever got out of that boat was constipation, dry hair, and scars on my shins from climbing those damn stairs to the top deck."

Ladder. It's a ladder to the bridge.

"And Leon spent more time fixing the damn thing than riding it. We had three places we went to: Oyster Bay, Lloyd Harbor, and Calf Island. That's as far as he could get. But he knew the plumbing and electric systems inside out. I hate to tell you what he paid for that thing, but he was too cheap to pay the boatyard for repairs, so he took a course in plumbing at the Adult School, can you imagine?" She shrugged. "Anyway, listen, I'll think about it, but ninety-nine to one I'm going with my bedroom. It's like my decorator says, simplicity is the biggest knockout. Now, where were we?"

"The music."

"Right. Okay, five and last: a makeup artist. The best. I want whoever does Dyan Cannon." She smiled coyly, expecting something. No one spoke. "Well, I look just like her, didn't you notice?"

"Of course." Margaret caught it before it bounced. "I was just thinking that her makeup sometimes looks a little . . . well, wouldn't you want a softer look? Younger? We can get her makeup person, of course, if that's what you want, unless he's out of the country on a shoot. Or if you like, we can try to get Roddy Agapalidou. Although he'd be a good deal more expensive than the other fellow, of course. No, never mind. We'll just do as you said, and—"

"Hold on. Roddy who? Why him?"

"Oh, you know, he's the one—people would give up their lovers before they gave up their place on his little list. They say he's like going to a plastic surgeon, only quicker. But he's a king's ransom and I'd have to pull a lot of strings to get you an introduction—"

"Does he do death?"

"I'm sorry?"

"Corpses. Anybody can do you when you're alive. Can he do me after?"

"I can't mention the name, but think of the most famous beautiful woman you know. She's paid him an outrageous amount to do her after she goes. You know, for the viewing."

"Get him."

"It's easier to get a private audience with the Pope, but I'll try."

"Try. Now, one last thing. The final pictures have to be taken before anybody gets there."

"Of course. You don't want your hair messed up."

"You got it."

"Trisha, one point we should clear up. When will the end be?"

"When do I die, you mean?"

"Yes."

Trisha shrugged happily. "When we've got a good take. When the director says it's a wrap. Then you do your stuff—poison dart or whatever—and clean up and get the hell out of there. It'll look like a heart attack or something?"

Margaret nodded.

"Perfect. I have to tell you, I am going to love this. He forgot about me? Let him forget this."

"You won't be there to enjoy it, you remember."

"I understand that. Hey, this is costing more than La Reserva. You think I don't know what I'm paying for?"

"Trisha, I think you always know exactly what you're buying," Margaret said with a tiny, admiring smile.

"Oh, you bet. Because I go to the best and I leave nothing to chance. I went to a therapist once who told me I had a control problem, I had to be in control of everything, and we were going to work on that and get me to give it up. I said, You got that half right, and I fired him. If he could afford to be in control of things he would be, too, instead of listening to everybody's shit at a hundred bucks an hour." She stretched. "Where do I sign?"

■ ■ ■

When Margaret returned from dropping Trisha back at her car, she was still smiling. Caroline grinned back at her. "You made that all up, about Roddy Whatshisname being so exclusive and about the famous beautiful woman who hired him to do her for the viewing. He's from Elizabeth Arden or somewhere, right?"

"You're getting too smart. Actually, he's very good with

her type of looks. And think how special she'll feel. Isn't that what it's all about?"

"Mm. You know what? I'm definitely going back to my exercise class. Every day, no matter what."

"I hope it has evening hours. I need you here."

Driving home, Caroline reran that sentence over and over, smug as a banker. She missed her exit and made two wrong turns before she got herself back on the Hutch heading home.

TEN

"LET ME HAVE two, three of them little soldiers, will you, honey? I hate to see 'em go into battle alone."

The stewardess reached underneath her cart, brought out three miniature bottles of Johnnie Walker Black, and lined them up on Charlie's tray table, one behind the other. "There you go," she chirped. "A whole battalion. You just sing out if you need reinforcements. Twist of lemon?"

"Hell, no, this ain't no pansy outfit. My troops here go down straight, and they go down fighting. Just a little ice for luck. Or don't you have ice cubes in Texas? Use hunks of a glacier imported from the Pole instead, do you?" Charlie was having a great time. He'd developed a Texas twang already. He nudged Caroline and winked at her.

"No, sir, we use regular ice cubes. It's the *other* kind of ice that comes in the big sizes in Texas. You know, diamonds? They don't bother with the little stuff a-tall. Just big old rocks." She set a whiskey glass on his table, and a tumbler full of ice. "I see some stones you wouldn't believe. How about you, ma'am? Some champagne for you today?"

"No, thanks. Could I have an iced tea?"

"Sure thing. You just give me a minute, okay?" She bestowed a napkin and a foil package of smoked almonds upon each of them and was gone.

"Nice girl," Charlie said. "Took right to me, too. I talk to 'em, kid 'em along."

"Better go easy with the drinks, Dad. You know it only makes the jet lag worse."

"Don't you worry, honey. These three little fellas don't even add up to a double. Takes more than that to make me lag. Hey, speaking of lagging, how's the old social life? You meeting lots of executives in your new place? Corporation guys planning parties?"

"I don't know. Not really. Their wives or their assistants mostly do the party planning. Listen, Dad, I wanted to tell you—I think you're doing great. You've had only one or two drinks a day all week. Haven't you?"

Charlie shifted around in his seat. "Sure, sure. Doing great. Hey"—he brightened—"you should've seen me take on Lindemayer last, uh, last . . . I dunno, Tuesday. I said, 'Lindemayer, my little girl is treating me to this thing nobody would believe,' and I told him the whole plan, beginning to end. We were waiting for our starting time, you know? So he says, 'Those new clubs going to have radar, Charlie? Help you locate the ball?' and I tell him I can beat him using a tree limb for a putter—you know, we're kidding around—hey, sweetheart?"

"Yes, sir? How you doing here?"

"You were right on the mark, honey, my troops here say they're outnumbered. Cavalry needs a li'l reinforcement. Backup, you know?"

The young woman's face betrayed surprise for a moment, then masked it. *You drank those so fast?* Caroline silently translated. Her spirits dipped; she hadn't even noticed that he'd polished off all three.

"Well, I'm fixin' to bring you a little dinner," the stewardess said cheerily. "How about you give me a chance to do that, then see if you still want those extra troops, okay? Don't want to drown the horses, do we?"

Charlie smiled broadly at her. "Hell, honey, those ain't horses, they're dragons. And they can *swim*. You bring me a Johnnie Walker Black and I'll remember you in my will."

Caroline tried to catch her eye, but the stewardess smiled and said, "Sure thing," and left.

"Dad—" Caroline began.

"Now, this is a special occasion, Pickle-pie. Don't go Dading me on a special occasion. Got to celebrate when somebody does a great thing for you, and I want to tell you this is one great thing you're doing. No, let me finish. That's just what I told Lindemayer, whose kids incidentally wouldn't give him a stepstool if he was hanging from a lamppost. I said, I got me a jewel of a daughter, Lindemayer, one honest-to-God gem. Kings and presidents live their whole lives and nobody gives 'em such a present." He cleared his throat.

Caroline put a hand on his arm. "So pace yourself a little, Dad. Don't get sick and spoil it all. I mean, to play at St. Andrews—"

"You're right." Charlie sat up straight in his seat and tucked in his chin. "You are dead right. I'm finished. Not a sip until tomorrow. Two a day, that's it. You be my good angel and remind me."

"You bet. And you know what? I bet you could do it forever. You'd feel so great, Dad." *I'll call Dr. Death off,* she thought for the thousandth time. *He'll just have his Moment and come home again. He can do it. I can help him do it.*

"Here you go." It was the damned stewardess, bearing a little tray with two more miniature bottles. Charlie looked regretfully at them and shook his head. "Change in tactics, honey," he said resolutely. "We're going to cut our losses here. That's how it is in combat, sometimes." He winked at her and let her go, and he gave Caroline a little salute, but then he looked gloomily out the window.

"Dad? How about Lindemayer?"

"What about him?"

"Did you beat him?"

"When? Oh, yeah. I beat him on the front nine." He drained his glass and set it down. The tremor in his hands was back. Caroline shifted gears, as she had done countless times before. She began jollying her father, keeping the beasts at bay with chatter and jokes and with details of the trip to Scotland. She paced herself; it was going to have to get them all the way to Texas.

■ ■ ■

"We look like Halloween." Janet picked up a piece of sushi with her chopsticks. She was wearing fluorescent hot-pink tights and a purple bodysuit. She had a hot-pink bandanna twisted around her head.

"Don't eat all the yellowtail. *You* look like Halloween; I look plain silly. But I kind of put it on sometimes—you know, for luck. Just when nobody's around."

"Thanks."

"You know what I mean. No . . . strangers. You should have seen him, Janet. He was so cute. We passed the shop—it was right there in the airport on the way to the gate, you know—and I didn't even see it, I was so busy trying to steer him away from the airport bar and get him to the gate. But he dragged me right in there. He only wanted to get me the whole outfit, chaps and all. It wasn't easy, but I held it down to just the hat." She smiled and put her hand up to touch the headband, suede and silver and turquoise. "He got one, too. Said he was going to wear it on the course at St. Andrews, put the fear of God into the Scots."

"I know. The reason I know is that you've told me all this twice before. Are you okay?"

"I just wonder how he's doing at Baltusrol. This is the trickiest time. I know it's idiotic, but I somehow think that if I wear this thing I can . . . I don't know . . . influence him? Keep him from—"

"Idiotic is definitely one of the words that come to mind. I can think of a few others. He's going to drink, Caroline, and you won't stop him with white magic or any other way. You never have."

"Maybe I should go and meet him there. Maybe—"

"You can't do that, and you know it. Didn't you just tell me that things are heating up and Margaret needs you four days a week? You want to risk her remembering that she can function without you?"

"No, but if—"

"Anyway, it always takes him months to get really sick, and it's only . . . what, a few weeks till Scotland?"

"Ten days."

"See, that's really soon. He'll be okay, even if he falls off the wagon. Look, you call him every morning, right?"

"Right."

"So far so good?"

"Uh-huh."

"So don't borrow trouble." Janet sat back and linked her hands behind her head. "Listen, I met somebody."

"Mm-hm." Caroline wasn't listening. She sat with her elbow on the table, a pair of chopsticks dangling from her hand. The hat sat a little askew on her head. Janet reached across the table, yanked the hat off Caroline's head, and set it down on the carpet. "Hello, testing. I said I *met* somebody."

"*What?* You didn't tell me."

"Did you ever try talking to an obsessive in a cowboy hat?"

"You met him at work?"

"No."

"Your aunt's friend's son. You said you weren't going to—"

"Not Alan the root-canal king. I haven't sunk that low."

"Is this twenty questions or are you going to tell me?"

"Promise you won't yell."

"Janet—"

"Say, 'No matter what, I will trust my friend Janet's judgment.' "

"No matter what, I will trust my friend Janet's judgment."

"You wouldn't have said that if you meant it."

"Fine. Don't tell me. I don't want to know. I don't want to hear it. Let me just ask you one thing: is he married?"

"Hardly." Janet smiled secretively and flushed. "Okay, okay. It's the guy who lives downstairs. Josh. The one that locks his bike up next to mine? Remember he helped me when I was trying to figure out which computer to get, and—"

"The *kid*?"

"He's not a kid. He's twenty-eight."

"And you'll be thirty-five in November." Caroline frowned, doing the math. "Janet, when you were starting college, this person was ten years old."

"Well, he isn't ten anymore. And he's incredible. He can cook. He does these gentle massages you wouldn't believe. He can *cry*." Janet was rosy and smug and foolish-looking.

"No wonder you've been going to aerobics every other minute," Caroline said sourly. "Last thing I heard, you were going to move to Texas where they'd appreciate your rear end."

"I'm getting appreciated just about all I can handle." Janet raised and lowered her eyebrows twice, like Groucho Marx. Caroline didn't respond. "I thought we agreed we weren't going to get desperate," she said.

"This is not desperate. You don't understand—it's *good* between us. Healthy, warm. He's sweet, Caroline. And he really cares about me. Anyhow, look who's talking. You still seeing Simon and his mustache?"

"On my terms."

"Which is to say whenever you get desperate."

"There are a lot of good things—"

"You sat in that very chair two weeks ago and tugged at your hair the way you've been doing when you were miserable since you were born, and you told me that he hisses when he gets romantic. He hisses and he uses the world's hokiest lines and he reminds you of Albert Knight from junior high, that's what you said. Caroline, the man is a wimp. He's afraid of his own kids."

"I know."

"So?"

"So I should ask Margaret's housekeeper Sarah to introduce me to one of her friends? They all give great massages, too. They're about twenty years old. I think you get arrested for that in this state, it's statutory—"

"Didn't you tell me you met somebody who came into the office? An accountant or something? What happened?"

Caroline shrugged. "Sarah let him in while I was alone in the office. He wanted Margaret, of course."

"Another humanitarian with a loved one to bump off," Janet said, dunking a piece of California roll into the soy sauce. "How adorable. Your kids will all be ax-murderers."

Caroline ignored her. "I was sitting on the floor, surrounded by mountains of paper. Those files . . . anyhow, I jumped up and said, 'Can I help you?' and he started talking about looking at Margaret's books, and I panicked. I thought he was the police or the IRS or something."

"That's not good. The feds come in, there goes the Graceful Exit, down the tubes."

"Please don't keep calling it that. It's Great Events. If you keep calling it the Graceful Exit, one day I'm going to answer the phone that way."

"Well, it's a much better name."

"Anyway, I got terrified and did my whole respectable-charming-small-party-business routine and I confused the hell out of him until finally we got it straight that he was Margaret's tax guy. Then I was embarrassed, but I still couldn't let him see the records without Margaret. I mean, I don't even know the combination to the safe where the books are. Anyway, she was due back in a couple of minutes, so we just chatted while we waited for her."

"Well? Is he interested?"

"I don't know. He said he wanted to have dinner one night."

"Aha! So?"

Caroline made a face. "He's one of those. 'Hi, I'm Chip Charming. I've been great-looking all my life and I play a sensational game of tennis, and I'll be glad to let you amuse me until a real contender comes along.'"

"What you mean is, he isn't broken and he isn't damaged, so you don't feel safe with him."

There was a long, tight silence. Caroline glared at her plate, eyes filling with tears. Just before it was too late, Janet grabbed Caroline's hand, curled in a fist around the chopsticks. "I'm sorry. I'm such an asshole—that was a real Dr. Bitch thing to say. Anyway, look who's talking, Miss Always-a-Bridesmaid. You've at least been married; you're the one who always has a man—"

"Simon is not a man. Simon is a twerp and you're absolutely right, I only see him when I'm desperate. I'm going to break it off." She got up and went into the bathroom. Janet could hear her blowing her nose. "It shouldn't be hard to do," Caroline said, returning to the table. "I'll just tell him it's me or the kids. He'll be gone on the next tricycle." She grinned shakily at Janet. "He'll just have to find someone else to hiss at."

"Atta girl. And Chip Charming?"

"Don't push it. Maybe I'll see him once, if he asks me. But I'm telling you, it isn't going to work. He wants a gorgeous, high-fashion—"

"Maybe. Or maybe he'll turn out to be a real person with feelings who's ready for a relationship."

"Maybe pigs will fly."

ELEVEN

SARAH KNOCKED AT the office door. Caroline was sitting on the couch, sorting papers. She held two articles on antique fire engines in her front teeth. "Hon in," she yelled.

Sarah poked her head into the room. "Did you say 'Come in'?" Caroline nodded, then released the two articles and laid them on the arm of the couch.

"Every third piece of paper in this place is going to have my toothmarks on it," she said. "What's up?"

"Delivery guy just brought this. Are we joining the circus or are Margaret and Mac getting into kinky sex? It definitely isn't for their kid." She was holding a box whose label showed a picture of a trapeze, and another that obviously contained a set of rings.

"Joining a circus. Or anyway a client is, sort of. This stuff must be for the party. You can, uh . . . how about putting it in the laundry room?"

"Roger. Too bad—I was rooting for kinky sex. Margaret is one cool bean, though; I wonder if she ever heats up."

Caroline wondered, too, briefly, then seized the opportunity to ask, "What about the daughter? What's she like?"

THE GRACEFUL EXIT

Sarah shrugged and ran a hand through her hair, holding it up away from her face. It was warm and humid for early May and she was wearing a royal blue tank top. There was a flat, silky starburst of dark hair under her arm. Caroline willed herself to remain expressionless and fixed her eyes on Sarah's face. "Whitney?" Sarah mused. "She's okay if you like rectangles."

"Rectangles?"

"You know. Straight lines and right angles, no surprises. Not as pretty as her mother, that's always tough, and a little ... hearty. I had a roommate like her for about a minute and a half in freshman year. Ginny Ann Burley. I didn't suit her at all, and she made my teeth hurt. I think she's growing up to be a lawyer. Anyhow, Whitney raises dogs and rides dressage and shit, and she comes in twice a year and lets Margaret dress her."

"Is she away at school?"

"Whitney is always away. Prep school, tennis camp, riding camp, ski week, college. When she comes home, she and Margaret smile and chirp for a day or so, then they get real and ignore each other except for shopping purposes."

"Does she do better with her father?"

"With Mac? Mac doesn't, like, *chat* with Whitney. He positions her. Whitney is being positioned for great things, poor little metepleecom."

"Mete . . . ?"

"Meat-Eating-Tennis-Playing-Economics-Major. A phrase left over from my co-op at Brown. Incredibly useful around here, except that nobody gets it."

"I eat meat," Caroline said. "I even play tennis. Somewhat."

"Yeah, but you're not a metepleecom. Metepleecoms don't do things somewhat—they're not here to play; they're here to win." She dismissed the subject with a mock shudder.

"Listen, thanks for telling me what to do with this stuff. I have to go fix lunch—my friend is coming over. Hey, you want to join us? She's a witch. Really spiritual. Calm, deeply calm. Every time I'm with her I feel peaceful for days. I'm making tabouli and cold carrot soup."

"That's really nice of you, but I can't. The whole point of my being here is for me to be *here*—answer the phones, catch the strays . . ."

"Woman's work," Sarah smiled. "Catch the strays and shape them up, answer the phones, keep it rolling. Think of it this way sometime: if just once you didn't answer this phone, would the universe be worse or better?" She swept out, bouncing the two boxes in her arms and making their contents jangle. The door slammed shut behind her.

Caroline was just putting the two fire-engine articles in a folder for Beneficiary Dickerman, who had a lifelong desire to drive a hook-and-ladder truck through town at high speed and to put out a raging fire with the guys, when the phone rang.

"Hello, Margaret?" said a sultry voice.

"This is her assistant."

"Oh, Charlotte."

"Caroline."

"Caroline, I'm so sorry. This is, uh, Lowell. Laura, really. Do you remember me?"

No, which transvestite who wanted to knock off his mother is this? "Of course I do. Laura, your voice sounds wonderful. So *female*. You've started the treatments?"

"You can tell," he purred. "Isn't it fabulous? The voice is the least of it. I'm thrilled. I'm really and truly thrilled. But listen, dear, I needed to ask Margaret something."

"Try me."

"Okay, sure. Here's the thing. I'm so nervous about

THE GRACEFUL EXIT

Wednesday and Thursday—I want it all to be perfect, you know?"

"Of course. How can I help?"

"Well, we'd figured that the passing would be sometime Thursday night, after the performance, but I've been thinking. I mean, it seems so *abrupt* that way. If it was later—late on Friday, say—then people could call her up on Friday and tell her how fabulous it was and she'd have a little chance to bask . . . " His voice trailed off.

Friday was out of the question. May seemed to be the busy season for assassinations; Dr. Death was booked to eliminate Beneficiary Goodfellow at the Golden Door in California on Friday. Caroline closed her eyes and conjured up her image of Lowell/Laura as a woman, red dress, enameled earrings and all. "We get this kind of question often, Laura," she began in a soothing, woman-to-woman tone, "and sometimes it does make sense to take the chance of putting off the passing."

"Take the chance?"

"Well, of course there's always the risk that something will happen the next day to wipe out all the pleasure of the Moment. With your mother, for example, you mentioned that there was a little rivalry between her and some of her guests."

"Stilettos at twenty paces is how I'd describe it."

"Right. Well, the night of the concert itself, they'll be all dressed up, and somehow that seems to make people behave."

"Oh, isn't that the truth."

"And they can't help being impressed—bowled over—by the whole evening; she'll see that. And they'll say lovely things and make a fuss over her. I think it's going to be a real triumph. But what about the next morning? You know how women can be. Mightn't someone who calls to thank her for the evening get in a little dig, or find a way to diminish the whole thing for her? It would be such a shame after all you've—"

"Carlotta Davis."

"That's the one with the son who's married to an investment banker?"

"Exactly. You remembered, aren't you something. Carlotta Davis will stay up all night sharpening a sentence, and in the morning she will use it to maim and destroy. Oh God, you're right. Do it Thursday night; it's the only way to keep the poor chickie safe. Seize the moment, as they say."

"Seize the moment."

■ ■ ■

Margaret didn't come in until five-thirty. Caroline was triumphant—she'd answered all the queries on the current client files, leaving the relevant clippings and neatly handwritten notes in each folder. She'd booked three flights, tracked down a used hook-and-ladder truck, and gotten two estimates for repainting it. She'd rented a sound stage, two pygmy elephants, and an aging tiger. And she'd handled Laura. She reported it all, flushed with pleasure, and only then noticed that Margaret was perturbed. "What's wrong?" she asked. "Should I have had Laura speak to you? I thought—"

"No, no, you did just the right thing."

"I might have overpaid a little for the tiger. I didn't know where else to call, though."

"What? Oh, poor old Rudolph's poor old tiger. No, don't be silly, we'll bill that right to Cecile. Things like tigers, you simply pay what they ask. No, you're fabulous. You're just fabulous, I mean it. I had a crummy afternoon, that's all."

"Another luncheon?"

"Family." She shaped the word like the name of a loathsome disease. "Sometimes I feel that I'm in exactly the right line of work. It'll be a pleasure to arrange for a few deaths, this afternoon. Preferably old men. Well. I think I'll trot in and phone up Dr. Gray." She rummaged through the papers on top of the desk. "Christ, where did I put this week's phone number? I thought I—"
"It's under the blotter."
"Don't lose another ounce at that exercise class of yours, Caroline; you're worth your weight in gold."
There was a tapping at the door. "Sarah?" Margaret called. Sarah opened the door. She'd changed; she was wearing all black—gauzy skirt, long tank top, and sandals that laced up her calves. Caroline could smell an insistent musky scent—perfume, she supposed. Sarah was dressed up. "I'm going," she declared. "There's a mess of pottage in the green bowl in the refrigerator."
"Where are you going?"
"Jennie's coven, remember? This is the night she invited me."
"Of course, full moon. I should have known."
"Your husband called. He has an unexpected dinner meeting. Back very late, he said. He'll be at Frankie and Johnnie's."
"Fine. Have a wonderful coven. Don't get involved with any warlocks."
Sarah smiled patronizingly and left. Margaret started toward the doorway, then turned back to Caroline. "Are you busy tonight? We could have dinner. Unless you—"
"That'd be great. I have no plans."
"Sevenish? That new place in Westport?"
"Sure. I'll book a table."
In fact, she had a date for dinner with two of the women from her old real estate office, but when Margaret left the

room she called and canceled it. She already knew all there was to know about Jean and Sandy; there were so many things to find out about Margaret.

* * *

Caroline twirled some angel hair pasta slowly on her fork. "If I called and asked Dr., uh, Gray how he was going to do it, I mean how my father is going to die, would he tell me?"
"Why would you want to know?"
"He said it was painless, but I . . . " She shrugged and ducked her head.
"He won't tell you."
"Do you know?"
"No."
Caroline knew at once it was a lie. Margaret knew; she knew everything about her business.
"But I know it's painless," Margaret went on. "Truly painless, Caroline." She poured another glass of wine for Caroline and one for herself. It finished the bottle. Caroline had never seen Margaret take a drink before. She seemed untouched by the alcohol. Margaret said, "He'll never see it coming; he'll never feel it. Ewen will be right there with him and you'll see, he'll tell us that your father fell suddenly asleep and didn't wake up. He leaves on the nineteenth?"
"Yes."
"Is he excited?"
"Very. I talked him out of taking his Princeton sweater; it's been too small for thirty years. Bought him tweedy knickers and a beautiful white Ralph Lauren sweater . . . he's planning on wearing that and his cowboy hat."
Margaret laughed. "I love his style. At least he doesn't sit around feeling sorry for himself."
"No, he—"
"Doesn't call you up and say he never sees you anymore

and you take him to lunch and he tells you how awful his life is and waits for you to fix it?"

Caroline shook her head.

"And then when you don't fix it because it's long since destroyed beyond repair, he doesn't make you feel as though you'd swallowed a snake?"

She was talking about her own life. Caroline sat motionless as a bird-watcher.

"You know what? Your father drinks and it's killing him, but at least he's a cheerful drunk. My mother was, too. She yelled and screamed and went up and down like a whaddayacallit—roller coaster—and she was totally useless as a mother, but at least she amused herself."

This was a bonanza. Once, on an otherwise disastrous date with a man who wore a gold bracelet, Caroline had gone to Atlantic City and played the slot machines. Early in the evening she had fed a quarter into a machine and won ninety-four dollars. She'd held the plastic coin container and watched the quarters bounce into the trough, stupefied, believing that each spurt was the last. She felt that way now, suddenly rich and greedy. She waited for more.

"My mother amused herself and you know what my father did? When she yelled he closed the windows, when she drove away the housekeepers he hired new ones, and all the time he pretended that nothing was wrong. What sorry bastards they are. They let themselves get manipulated and used, sweep it all under the rug, and then wake up when it's too late, whining that they want a life and don't know how to get one."

"I'm sorry. You've had a hard time." *More. Tell me more.*

"Well, who hasn't. Anyway, I got a business out of it—that's more than most do."

"What do you mean?"

"My first . . . someone I knew very well a few years ago

had an alcoholic father. That's what we had in common, I guess. Anyway, I didn't know much that was useful, but I did know how to give a party. I helped my friend to arrange a drop-dead party for his father's birthday, and that's just what it turned out to be. The old fellow had such a good time at his party that he dropped down dead in the sorbet. My friend had the most amazing reaction: he was delighted. He kept saying, 'Thank God he was so happy when he died. He was with everyone he cared about—it was just the way he'd have wanted to go.' At the time, Mac was looking for a business for me, and it just clicked. I didn't tell him what I had in mind, of course. All I said was, 'How about party planning?' Mac put up the seed money and I took it from there."

"How did you find Dr. Death? Gray. Dr. Gray."

Margaret smiled distantly and motioned to the waiter to bring the check. "Enough stories for you. You'll have bad dreams." It was a fiat. They made small talk as they walked out to the parking lot. They were waiting for the valet to bring their cars when Caroline suddenly asked, "Did you used to try to do wonderful things for your mother? Make her happy?"

Margaret stretched her neck in a slow circle, eyes closed. The coach lights shone off her blond hair. "Make Mommy glad and she'll stop getting drunk and be a regular mother? Sure, I tried it. It worked great."

"It did?"

"Yup. The last time."

Caroline's car pulled up. They said a quick good-night and she got in and drove slowly out of the graveled parking lot. She could feel the words shooting around through her veins, an electric bulletin: *Yup. The last time.*

There was a thin, glossy little magazine that appeared monthly in every realtor's office and doctor's and dentist's waiting room in Westchester, outlining the month's events and focusing on local celebrities, social events, businesses, and entrepreneurs. Driving the highway with the windows open, Caroline imagined them interviewing Margaret for a feature article, "Focus on Margaret X." "What a stunning idea," she heard the interviewer coo, an overdressed, sharp-faced woman who was taking in the sight of Margaret's overflowing lavender file cabinets and avidly assessing her net worth. "Will you tell us how you came to think of so unique a concept as Great Events?" And Caroline saw Margaret—sitting in simple elegance behind her desk, wearing her ivory silk blouse with the stock tied high at her throat—look thoughtfully at the interviewer and then answer, "Well. I had to do something about Mother."

TWELVE

IT WAS MAY 17. The back doorbell rang. Caroline, sitting at the desk, said into the telephone, "Mrs. Griffiths, could you hold on for just a moment?" Half expecting to find Libby and her pulverized mom, she opened the door warily. It was Chip Charming. "Hi," he smiled. "Rob Gerard, remember me?"

She stumbled a little, backing up to let him in. "Of course. Please come in. Margaret said you'd be here sometime today. She's detained at a luncheon, but she left the books for you." She was blushing. *Cool it,* she instructed herself brusquely. *Serene smile. I'm in control here.* "Give me a minute to get off the phone and I'll show you a quiet place to work, all right?"

"Great." He had a 101-degree smile, slightly above body temperature. She left him standing in the middle of the room and hurried back to the phone, thinking, *Don't walk into the desk, Caroline.*

"Mrs. Griffiths? I'm so sorry. What I was telling you was that unfortunately, we don't, uh, arrange events for pets. . . . No, I can appreciate that. I know, sometimes they are more human than people. . . . Uh-huh, but . . . Uh-huh. That's hard, that's really hard. . . . No, I'm really sorry, we just can't take it on. We're not equipped, we're just not knowledgeable

THE GRACEFUL EXIT

enough to do the kind of job you'd want." She glanced at Rob Gerard. He was grinning. "Mrs. Griffiths? I do have a suggestion for you. Well, if Chumley is that sociable, I think I remember hearing Pegeen Fitzgerald on the radio, talking about a retirement home for pets. It was called the Last Post or something. I mean, my dog would have loved that. It would have been a continual party, as far as he was . . . oh, just a mutt. Mostly shepherd, we thought. . . . Yes, why don't you? He really might. You're very welcome. I hope it works out for you and Chumley. Oh, and don't mention our service to Mrs. Fitzgerald, will you? We like to keep our client list to a few special . . . Uh-huh. I knew you'd understand. Goodbye. You keep well."

"Fantastic." Rob Gerard flashed a Rhett Butler grin at her. He was really good-looking. Longish sandy hair, great square jaw, smile lines at the corners of his eyes, perfect teeth. Perfect equanimity. All the world his mirror. "She wanted to give a formal dinner dance for her dog before he got too old to tango?"

"I never got far enough to find out what event she had in mind for Chumley. Can you believe it? A dog?" She laughed, a squeaky little chortle she'd abandoned in high school. The sound brought her up short, appalled. *Waiting for him to ask you to the prom, Caroline?* Embarrassed and furious at herself, she said, too briskly, "Well, let me get you started. Margaret suggested that you work in the library. I'll just . . ."

Margaret had taken two blue ledgers out of the safe and locked them in the desk drawer. Now Caroline took them out. Holding them cradled in her arm like schoolbooks, she ushered Rob Gerard into the library. She laid the ledgers down on the leather-topped desk. Just as she was leaving, he said, "You know, when I made this appointment with Margaret, I was going to call you and ask if you'd have dinner with me tonight, but I was scared you'd turn me down." A bashful smile, this time. *Liar,* Caroline thought. *You've never been scared to ask anyone out in all your life. What happened was, you forgot I existed until I opened the door for you.* "But could you?" he asked. "Just on the spur of the moment?"

She had the sentence all framed: "Oh, I'm so sorry"—a little shocked, a little patronizing—"I'm busy this evening." But she thought of Janet. *He isn't broken and he isn't damaged, so you don't feel safe with him.* In defiance she smiled a cool and easy smile, just like Cookie McIlhenny, the most popular girl in the eighth grade. "Sure," she said, as though it meant as little to her as it did to him. "Why not? Just someplace local, though. I'm not dressed . . . "

In fact she was wearing her new natural silk pants and a silk and linen sweater Janet had made her buy, and she thought she looked pretty good. He turned another dazzler on her. "You look too good," he said glibly. "Anyway, around here people go out in business clothes all the time, jeans, anything. That'll be fine."

Smiling stiffly and wishing she'd said she was busy, she turned to leave. The leather wing chair in the corner made her think wistfully of Dr. Death. Now there was a man. Not broken and not phony either. Kind, intuitive, understanding. Dr. Death liked her just the way she was. He thought she was brave and generous and caring and that was what he valued . . . That and having the desire and the means to have a loved one bumped off. She shrugged bitterly and went back to work, thinking, *Men.*

■ ■ ■

When Margaret walked in an hour or so later, she had someone with her. "Caroline, I want you to meet Sam Ross," she said. "Sam's a city person. He thinks there are bears in the woods here in Greenwich. Sam, this is Caroline Mayhew, my partner."

THE GRACEFUL EXIT

"Hi," Sam said. He looked gloomy and preoccupied. He was wearing jeans, a corduroy jacket, and a button-down blue shirt with a knit tie. He had thinning curly black hair, graying in the front, and sharp blue eyes.

"I admire your courage," Caroline said, trying to put him at ease.

He looked at her warily. "Why?"

"You came out here without so much as a rifle or mosquito netting." Margaret looked at her in surprise. She was always surprised when Caroline made a joke.

"I had my shots," Sam said. "And I've got my switchblade, of course. Wore boots, too, in case of snakes." He hiked up one jeans leg. He did have boots on, well broken in cowboy boots with flat heels. Caroline smiled. He smiled back, but he looked miserable. He glanced at Margaret.

"All right," she said. "Sam has a train to catch, so we'd better get started. Sit down, Sam. That couch is comfortable. Coffee? No? Then tell us about Harold."

"Harold is a prince," he said. He sighed and rubbed a hand over his mouth. "Special. The man is a scholar and a gentleman in a world full of ignorant thugs."

"What does he do?" Margaret prompted.

"Newspaperman. He's had a regular byline at the *Times* forever—outlasted everybody there, just about. Writes pieces for *The Nation* from time to time. One of the best. His stuff is sharp, totally accurate. Elegant. In fact, he's an elegant man." He was smiling a little now, looking into the middle distance, seeing Harold. "Not a dandy, God knows—he has jackets that must go back to Harry Truman—but elegant like a perfect math problem: everything fits and everything works. He is exactly who he is, no spare gestures, no padding."

Sam loved this man Harold, and he was sitting there writing his obituary. Caroline swallowed hard.

"Harold plays sensational pool and suicidal poker, and he's insanely addicted to both. Between them he just about breaks even. No heirs and no assigns. What else would you like to know? Oh, and he taught me everything he knew, which I was then too chicken to use."

"Didn't you say you were an editor?" Margaret queried.

"Books, lady, I edit books. This is to being a newspaperman as crocheting is to surgery. I didn't have it. I simply wasn't *fast* enough. Harold saw—sees—things instantly and completely, and then he starts looking deeper, and while he's looking he's composing, and what he composes hardly ever needs a rewrite. I see something on Monday—Wednesday I begin to figure it out, Friday I'm ready to write a first draft. With luck. Anyhow"—he sat forward and planted both feet on the floor—"I want to throw him a party. There are two things Harold would love. One involves a boat"—he raised his eyebrows in a private gesture of dismissal "—and the other is fit for humans. You know that island in Vermont that Woollcott and the Round Table group used to have?"

"Benchley and Dorothy Parker and all of them?"

"Yeah, they spent summer weekends there for years. They had a rule, no married couples could come together. They swam and played badminton and croquet and kibitzed and—who knows what they did, you get the picture."

"Summer camp," Caroline said.

"Right. So there are maybe eleven or twelve guys—a couple of them are girls ... *women* ... he's close to. Poker buddies, pool victims, just about all of them writers. I want you to find that island, rent it, stock it with a lot of food and booze—"

"And badminton birdies and decks of cards," Caroline put in.

"Yep. Water wings, a couple of boats, and some fishing

lines. Good cigars. I'll give you a list. A cook, I guess, and somebody to clean up, maybe, but otherwise leave us the hell alone and then on Sunday in the late afternoon, put him to bed." He looked hard at Margaret to make sure she understood. She nodded.

"Why?" Caroline asked. "What's wrong with him?"

"I'll tell you a story. Two stories. One about keys and one ... not about keys. You know the parking garage under Lincoln Center?"

"Sure."

"Okay, so you know that you park your own car there. It's park and lock."

"Uh-huh."

"We went to a concert there in January."

"You drove?" Margaret asked. "I thought city people took cabs."

"Newspapermen take cabs rarely, subways sometimes. Mostly they run. But sometimes you have to go to bizarre places for a story—other boroughs, Connecticut even—and it's quicker and cheaper to drive. In fact, Harold despises public transportation, so he drives a lot. He keeps a police radio in the car, too, which you can't do on the subway. A lot of the guys do. Anyway, I meet him at this concert—upstairs in the lobby—and when it's over we come down to the garage and suddenly he stands still with this look of sick panic on his face. I'm saying what is it, what's wrong? No answer. Then finally he reaches into his pocket, looking like death, and he pulls out this gizmo and pushes a button on it. Then he looks around and yanks at my arm, saying, 'Come on.' And he drags me right to it."

"The car?"

"The car. There are always horns sounding in those garages, right? But I realize, as he's pulling me along, that there's a horn that isn't stopping and that we're getting closer and closer to it. That was *his* horn."

"I don't understand."

"The horn was blowing and the headlights were going on and off like crazy. That was what happened when he pushed the button on the gizmo. It makes your car horn sound and the lights flash so you can find where you left it. A hundred dollars from some mail-order place. He spent a hundred bucks on a device to tell him where he parked his car because he *knows* he can't count on remembering."

"Everybody forgets things," Caroline offered softly.

"Harold forgets nothing. He's a great reporter because he's fast and alert and because every goddamned fact that ever flashed by him got stuck, categorized, and filed. Our elected fuckups are terrified of him because they know that every word they ever said is on file." He tapped his head. "In there."

"What's the other story?" Margaret asked.

Sam ran a flat hand up from the nape of his neck and down over his forehead. "Horsefish," he said wretchedly. "We were talking about one of the presidential candidates and he said, 'Well if I'm any judge of horsefish . . . ' " He looked significantly at them, as though that clinched it. They looked back at him, waiting for more. He rolled his eyes. "Horsefish?? It's horse*flesh*. The saying is, If I'm any judge of horseflesh. He said horsefish. I tell you, when I heard that, my gut rode the express elevator. Down."

"Maybe he was tired, or had had too much to drink," Caroline tried.

Sam shook his head. "That was just the beginning. He's been doing it a lot. More and more. His words are leaving him. He's repeating himself and forgetting things and not being able to finish sentences. I didn't tell you everything, either, things going on at home. Finally I read a book about

Alzheimer's, and it's all there. Senile dementia, what a hideous phrase."

Caroline glanced at Margaret, who was nodding soberly. "Harold is dead," Sam said angrily, "and I'm not going to let him rot in public. He'd never forgive me."

Dr. Death's going to love him, Caroline thought. *The perfect client.* She wondered, for a moment, whether Dr. Death had any prejudices against gays, then dismissed the idea as unworthy. But the thought of Dr. Death reminded her that Rob Gerard was in the library. Margaret and Sam were discussing details of Harold's Moment, so she waited. It was clear that this was going to be a major extravagance for Sam Ross, but as they talked about the weekend, he relaxed and even brightened a bit, and when finally Margaret brought him around to the phone conversation with Dr. Gray, he stood up and said, "Let's do it."

"Rob Gerard stopped by," Caroline murmured to Margaret. "He's working in the library."

"Well, we'll just move him," Margaret said briskly. "Let me have a minute; I'll settle him in the living room, and then I'll come down for Sam."

Caroline, left with Sam, said, "I like your boots. I have a cowboy hat, but I never wear it outside my apartment."

Sam grinned crookedly. "You go home and put it on like bedroom slippers? Your bedroom hat?"

"Kind of. I'd feel dumb wearing it anyplace else."

"Did your oil-magnate uncle send it to you with the proviso that if you wear it so many hours a day you'll inherit the ranch?"

"I wish. My father got it for me."

"Oh, boy. I know how that is. My mother went to see the original production of *Ain't Misbehavin'*. They were selling this jacket in the lobby, apparently—a yellow satin team jacket? On the back where it ought to say, 'Murray's Plumbing Supplies,' it says, 'Ain't Misbehavin'.' In purple. And then across the bottom it says, 'One Never Knows, Do One?' "

Caroline laughed.

"Actually it's a great jacket, but where the hell am I going to wear it? So it hangs there in the hall closet. Listen, it could have been worse. She went to Mexico once and brought my sister a crocheted bikini. In her best moment, my sister was never a candidate for a bikini, let alone this little string affair. I live in dread that she'll go to Switzerland—"

"Lederhosen!"

"You got it. My worst nightmare. With one of those little shirts? And the hat?"

Margaret appeared at the door. Sam squared his shoulders and winked sadly at Caroline. "My rendezvous with destiny," he said, and he followed Margaret into the library.

Caroline was standing in front of the tile-framed mirror, trying to wink, when Margaret came back into the office. "Caroline, can you drive Sam to the station?" she asked. "I have at least an hour's work with Rob, and—"

"Sure. No problem. Margaret?"

"Yes?"

"Can Sam afford to use us?"

Margaret looked startled, as though Caroline had asked whether she was wearing underwear. "Of course. Not easily—editors make nothing—but he can do it. He has no kids, no wife, no ex-wife. Seems to live a quiet life. So he has enough. These are the ones I like best, in fact." She smiled indulgently. "They *savor* their Moments more than others do. It's not just another little frippery to them. Anything else?"

"No. Yes. What's Rob like?"

"Rob? Oh, he's safe. First of all he's an accountant, and they never talk. They're like priests, only shiftier. And sec-

THE GRACEFUL EXIT

ondly, he has no idea. He figures people in this area pay fortunes for everything else, why not for parties? So not to worry. See you later."

■ ■ ■

Sam and Sarah converged on the office a few minutes later. "Mr. Gerard says he'll be held up for an hour or so, and do you mind if dinner is a bit late?" Sarah said.

"No, tell him that's fine." Noticing Sarah looking curiously at her, she added, "Talk about your metepleecoms." Sarah exited laughing.

"Is that a word I'm supposed to know?" Sam asked as they got into Caroline's car. She pulled her map of Greenwich out of the glove compartment and found the railroad station. Frowning, she plotted her way to it. "Metewhatsis?" Sam persisted. "Is it common parlance and I've lost it, like Harold? Maybe I'd better arrange a twofer."

"No, don't do that. It's a word Sarah made up. Meteplee-com: Meat-Eating-Tennis-Playing-Economics-Major. It happens to fit this person I'm having dinner with. Chip Charming. He scares me to death." She'd snuck a look at Sam's face when he emerged from the library; he didn't look as though he'd been crying but she chattered along anyway, offering up anything that came to mind, to distract him.

"What part scares you," he inquired, gamely joining in the banter. "The meat, the tennis, or the economics?"

"The charming. Damn it."

"What?"

She pulled the car over to the curb and was checking the map. "No, hey, I'm right, actually. Look at that! Two more stop signs and *then* veer off to the left." She drove on, still clutching the map.

"You new around here? Don't for God's sake lose me in the briar patch."

121

"Not new, just congenitally lost. But don't worry, I've got it now."

"Uh-huh. I knew this would happen if I went north of Ninety-sixth Street. What are our chances? You got a canteen? Some beef jerky?"

"... now veer to the *left*... a block ahead... Aha! Right there, big as life. You even have time to watch the females feeding their young." She pointed toward the Häagen-Dazs on the corner, where several little bunches of grade school children hopped around eating ice cream cones, flanked by pairs of young mothers.

"I saw this in *National Geographic*. It's terrifying in the flesh. So what's with you, you don't like charming?"

"I'm afraid of it. I don't know whether to believe anything one of those superappealing types says. You know?"

"Oh, yes, I know. So how come you're going out with him?"

"I—whoops, there's your train." She put a hand on his arm. "I hope things go well I hope Harold's weekend is everything you want it to be."

He nodded and got out of the car. When he reached the platform, he turned around to see whether she was still there. He looked forlorn, but he pantomimed looking through a pair of binoculars at the group in front of Häagen-Dazs. She smiled at him and winked. It was a clumsy wink, involving the whole right side of her face, but it made her feel warm and suave, and she drove off still smiling.

■ ■ ■

"How do you know he's gay? Superflaming, or did he tell you, or what? Look at this." Janet held up a black silk jumpsuit. "You could wear this."

"To what? Anyway, no black. We try to avoid—"

"Of course. No black in the offices of Drop-Dead Affairs.

But there is a life outside of work, you know, and sometimes you wear clothes in it. Now, what about this Sam?"

"He's not flaming or even . . . you know . . . but he's thin and nice-looking and single—never been married—and he's doing this for his friend. Male friend."

"Best friend from high school?"

"Older man. I think they share an apartment. They go to concerts and things together."

"Well, that could just be—"

"Besides, do you know what this Moment is costing him?" She mentioned a round figure.

"You're right. He's gay. Well, for Christ's sake, don't touch him."

"Jesus, Janet. You'd have burned witches, too."

"I would not. I'd have made damned sure not to get barbecued myself, though. Ooh, look at this." She held up a green silk dress with a halter back and a deep V cleavage. "Josh loves me in revealing things."

"That's the ticket, then. Reveals everything but your tax returns."

"Come on, and bring those things. I want to see you in the jumpsuit."

In the dressing room, wriggling through the green sheath, Janet asked. "So? How was it with Chip Charming?"

"Long."

"Long, as in you saw him off after breakfast with a satisfied, rosy glow?"

"Long, as in 'How soon is the waiter going to bring the coffee so I can go home?' I tried, Janet. I had on the natural silk pants and the sweater—"

"Thank you, Janet."

"Thank you, Janet, and I looked okay, and I guess he liked me. I mean, we talked a lot and he'd been to school with some people I knew and he kept saying these things—"

"What things?" Janet turned her back so Caroline could zip up the dress, then turned again and fixed her with a businesslike look. "What things?"

"Oh, you know, 'Next time we'll have to find a place with a band,' and 'Don't blush if you expect me to keep my distance. I make like Clark Gable when a girl blushes.' "

"Woo hoo!"

"Yuck."

"Uh-huh. I notice you committed it to memory."

"He meant me to. He meant for me to sigh into my pillow and . . . It's a game, Janet. I can just tell. He does this for sport. Anyway, I couldn't focus on him. I kept thinking about my father." Caroline had sat down on the little chair in the corner of the dressing room, a pile of clothing in her lap. She was pulling distractedly on a strand of hair.

"He leaves tomorrow?"

"The night flight to London. I'm taking him out for an early dinner and then out to Kennedy. Janet?"

Janet looked at her in the mirror.

"Are you buying that dress?"

"I don't know. You like it?"

"It's fine. Listen, if you're going to buy it, could you do it and let's go? I want to go home."

"Okay, honey. Want to stay at my place tonight?"

"No, Dad might call."

"Want me to stay over? We could rent a movie and eat everything in the house."

"No, I'm okay. I just want to go home."

"You'll do anything to keep from trying on that jumpsuit."

"Right."

■ ■ ■

"Did I tell you how cute you look in that hat?"

THE GRACEFUL EXIT

"Yes, Dad. You told me, and you told the waiter and the coat-check girl, and the person at the baggage check-in . . ."

"Well, you do. If I'd a known how cute you'd look, I'd a sent to Texas twenty years ago for one."

"You look great in yours, too. Everyone'll think you're a Texas millionaire."

"Right up until they see my swing. Then they'll think I'm Gary Player."

"Got your tickets?"

"Right here."

"Passport?"

"Check."

"Don't forget, when you get to London, you have to zip right on over to the connecting flight."

"Pickles, I'm going to fly there without a plane. This is just the greatest thing. I only hope I don't disgrace myself. Hey, no kidding now, a real duke and duchess?"

"No kidding. And Margaret says you can beat them at bridge, too. What's wrong? Why are you taking those?"

"Little gas. Heartburn, whatever. Say, look, they've got a lounge here. Let me buy you a cup of coffee. No, c'mon we've got a minute. Coffee for you, little beer for me. You know that the best thing to settle your stomach is a glass of beer? Truth."

"Dad, they're boarding. They've called first class already. That's you."

"La-di-da. I'm so fancy, I don't know myself."

"Take your raincoat."

"Yup. Well, here goes, then."

"Here, keep all these together. Have a great time. Enjoy every second of it, okay? I love you."

"Hey, no crying. I oughta be crying; I'm the one with the lousy stance and the unfixable slice. Don't know why you insist on loving this old wreck, but I love you, too. Hey, by the time I get back, you latch onto a fella. Deal?"

"Deal."

"Bye."

He waved and was gone, flourishing his hat and bowing stiffly to the stewardess at the boarding gate, then disappearing from sight.

THIRTEEN

CHARLIE MAYHEW WAS happily getting snorked when the pilot came on and began talking rapidly about seat belts and flotation devices. Charlie didn't pay much attention, even when there was the commotion in the aisle. To tell the truth, he was pretty far gone. The explosion, when it came, was a surprise to him, but in the nature of a distant surprise. The last thing he did was to grab for his Johnnie Walker Black, as he and it slid and lurched and entered the earth's atmosphere together.

FOURTEEN

CAROLINE THOUGHT IT was the alarm, but the ringing didn't stop when she groped for the button and pushed it. Not the alarm. So she picked up the phone, blinking in the darkness. What time? Five-fifteen? The dial tone sounded blandly in her ear. Not the alarm, not the phone. She fumbled the receiver back onto its cradle and, wrapping her arms around herself, lurched toward the front door. "Who is that?" she demanded.

"It's me, honey. Janet."

"Janet?"

"Open the door, Callie."

Janet never called her that, not in the last fifteen years. Peter called her that. She undid the locks, opened the door and stood back, squinting against the light that assaulted her from the hallway. "What is it?" she demanded. "What's the matter?"

"Were you asleep? Did I wake you up?"

Janet was dressed. She had on jeans and a shirt and she was carrying an overnight bag. "*Yes*. Of course you—"

"Oh, thank God. You haven't—nobody called?"

"What? Could you come in? I'm freezing. What's wrong?" Janet closed the door and locked it and took Caroline's hand. She led her back to the bedroom. "Get into bed," she commanded. "Get warm. Move over, let me sit. Listen honey, there's very bad news. I didn't want them to . . . I wanted to tell you myself." She laid a hand on the bump under the quilt that was Caroline's arm. "Your dad's plane. There was, um, an accident." Janet was crying. "An explosion, they think maybe a bomb. They're looking for the black box, but—"

"Dad?"

Janet shook her head. "No one survived," she whispered.

Caroline didn't move at all. She said something.

"What?"

"I'll have to cancel at Elizabeth Arden."

No one moved. Then Caroline said, "Janet?"

Janet waited.

"You're sure?"

"It's been on the radio and TV for . . . I guess it's almost an hour now. We were up, and we heard it on the news, so I checked and—"

"It's five-something. You were up?"

Janet shrugged sheepishly.

"Oh." She tried to smile, then her face twisted and she wailed. She turned over and buried her face in the pillow and flailed at the bed like a child. Janet waited.

■ ■ ■

"Dr. Gray?"

"Yes?"

"This is Caroline. Margaret said I should—"

"Oh, yes, Caroline. How are you doing?"

"Okay. Better. Funny, it's not like I wasn't expecting it. *Planning* it. But—"

"Oh, but to have it taken from your hands, and in such an ugly way. They think it was a bomb, I understand."

"Yes. And I wanted to know—"

"How it was for him."

She nodded, then said, "Right."

"How was he when he left?"

"He took some Maalox just before he boarded. Gas, he said."

"We know it was more than gas. He'd been drinking pretty heavily again?"

"I don't know. I guess so. He really wanted a beer before the flight."

"Mm-hmm. You've flown with him recently?"

"Yes, we went—"

"Did he take a drink during the flight?"

"Three, before we'd even leveled out. He only stopped because I stopped him."

"Caroline, do you think he ever flew without having a drink or two?"

"No. Never."

"More than two or three, if you weren't there to stop him?"

"Oh, yes. Much more, I think."

"So the odds are that he was pretty much out of it when the explosion occurred, isn't that right?"

"I guess."

"Would you like to know how it probably was?"

"Mm-hmm," she hummed, too high.

"If he hadn't passed out from the alcohol, he was certainly in an extreme state of, uh, sedation. Most likely all he felt was the last . . . the explosion. And that would have been so sudden, and so complete. The pressure, you know. Instantaneous. And with the way he was beginning to feel again, even if he'd made it to Scotland he might well have deteriorated so quickly that his Moment would have been less than perfect."

"I waited too long."

"You gave him excitement and anticipation and the knowledge that he was loved. Could anyone have done more? And *would* you have done it any sooner?"

"No."

"I'm sorry for you, Caroline, that your picture of his last minutes has been so marred. But for him—he probably went in the best possible way. Everything to look forward to, tipsy as a lord, no pain."

"Yes."

"Yes." He waited for a long, therapeutic moment, then in a slightly less intimate tone said, "But what a world we live in. Grenades in airports, bombs on planes. Animals. No regard for life, no regard at all."

He sounded for all the world like a butler in one of the great houses, decrying the lack of gentility among the help at McDonald's. Despite herself, Caroline felt her mouth quirk into a grin. It was her first smile in days.

■ ■ ■

Six o'clock. Caroline was sitting hunched over a cup of coffee, wearing disreputable jeans, her most comfortable sweatshirt and the cowboy hat, trying to deal with Charlie's bills. He'd had his own idiosyncratic system of bookkeeping, involving complex and cryptic notations, and more than once, stymied and maddened, she'd started to the phone to call him and tell him to decipher them himself. She was hot on the trail of his last several doctors' bills and the attendant medical insurance paperwork when the buzzer rang. Janet? Did they have a date tonight? Still holding the yellow and pink forms, she depressed the speaker button. "Yes?" she asked.

"Caroline? It's Sam Ross."

Sam Ross. Who was Sam Ross? She stood in confusion, finger poised over the buzzer. Suddenly she remembered.

"Hi, Sam! Hold on, I'll buzz you . . ."

On the way to the door, she remembered to take off the hat. She tossed it onto the hall table and pushed up her sleeves. One slid down immediately.

Sam Ross, wearing something yellow and shiny and holding a rectangular object wrapped in tinfoil, stood in the hallway. "You look like hell," he said. "Here. I brought you a casserole."

"You—how come?"

"I don't know. Somebody dies, you bring a casserole. I never asked why. I was going to call and ask if it was all right to come by, but I was afraid you'd say no and I'd be stuck with all this chicken and rice. I figured you might have people dropping by this week . . ."

He politely didn't look past her, but it was obvious that there was no one in the apartment but her.

"No. No one here but me."

"Thank God. Can I come in?"

She stepped back apologetically and he walked past her, looked around, located the kitchen, and put the casserole down. As he turned away from her, she saw the writing on his jacket: *AIN'T MISBEHAVIN'*.

"Caroline, I'm sorry—"

"You wore it!"

"Yeah. I thought it would cheer you up. I hope you appreciate it; it was the ultimate gesture of derring-do. I mean, there might have been *people* here."

"You wore it on the train?"

"Are you kidding? I drove. On dark streets. And *then* I parked as close to your house as I could get, and walked kind of with my back to the buildings."

"Did you drive Harold's car?"

He nodded. "He's not using it much these days. I listened to the police radio all the way up. There's a drug bust in Riverdale and domestic mayhem in Yonkers. Listen, I'm so sorry about your father."

"How did you know?"

"I talked to Margaret yesterday. I asked for you and she mentioned that your father had been on that flight to London. I thought of the hat. Are you okay?"

"Yes. I mean, I keep forgetting why I'm crossing the street and what I'm doing in the supermarket and things like that, but every day it's a little easier. Why were you asking for me?"

"Oh, I don't know. I had some questions and you're easy to talk to."

"Second thoughts?"

"Oh, that. Every hour on the hour, but that's no big deal. I have second thoughts about everything—do I really want raisin bran for breakfast? Am I happy with Hanes, or should I switch to Fruit of the Loom?—so it's only to be expected that when I plan a . . . you know, the M word . . . I'll be ricocheting off the walls. No, I just wanted to check on some things, but that can wait. Now, how about Aunt Adele's chicken and wild rice with mushrooms?"

"Your aunt made this?"

"My God, I hope not; Aunt Adele's been gone these twenty years. That's just the name of the recipe—Aunt Adele's Chicken and Rice with Mushrooms. In my family we footnote everything: Cousin Phyllis's herb dip, Carol's friend Barry's joke about the French Olympic swimmer, Great-grandma's hazel eyes that skip a generation. This is my rendition of Aunt Adele's recipe. It needs to be heated up."

"I can't believe you made this for me."

He shrugged. "You were nice to me on the worst day of

my life. So far. First you tried to find another way out for Harold, even though you're in the business of arranging, uh, final solutions. Then you joked and kidded with me all the way to the train, because you saw how destroyed I was. And I get the feeling that you're not a natural kidder. And then you sat there in your car, smiling at me until the train pulled out. I was really touched by that. You can't know how terrified I was, coming to that meeting. I mean, just imagine it. A thousand times I decided not to come at all. And then by the time I left, it was okay. I mean, I was wretched, but I knew Harold was in caring hands. Yours as well as mine."

"How is it now?"

He put two thumbs up. "Things will work out," he said cheerily.

She recognized it with a shock: it was her talisman. "Do you believe that?" she asked tactlessly.

"No. I'm a pessimist, by birth and by training—I say it to fool the gods. I keep hoping they'll take it as a stage direction."

"I say it, too! Just that way! I'm always saying it to myself when everything looks blackest. So far it hasn't fooled anybody but me."

"Tell me about things looking black."

While the casserole heated in the oven, she set the table and told him about Peter, surprising herself. It seemed the only thing to do; she couldn't bring herself to tell him about her father, and his pain about Harold seemed so enormous that she couldn't offer anything puny in exchange. It wasn't the kind of thing she'd ever tell a man, normally, but of course Sam was different—he wasn't in the running at all. It was easy, actually, telling him.

"The man has to be a grade A jerk," he said quietly when she'd finished. "I could have told you not to mess around with sailors."

THE GRACEFUL EXIT

"Are you into boating?"

He looked affronted. "I am not. The very idea makes me nauseous. It's not hard enough when the world holds still—I'm going to purposely put myself in a situation where everything's rocking and rolling but me? Uh-uh. Well. You've surely found someone far better than him by now."

It was a question. She smiled noncommittally and served the casserole, suddenly feeling that she'd told him enough to balance out Harold, and unwilling to admit how pathetic her love life was. The chicken was good, homey and savory, if a little overcooked. She smiled to herself at her stereotyped expectation of what a gay man would bring for dinner—something spare and exotic, exquisitely arranged on a square Japanese dish with a hibiscus blossom in one corner. This was in a Pyrex baking dish with a chip out of one handle. There was going to be enough left over for at least two more meals.

They picked at the leftover casserole and told each other stories. They found a pint of Heavenly Hash in the freezer and polished it off. He spotted the hat and admired it. She told him about her father in the airport shop, and then about the mixed blessings of shopping with Janet, which made him laugh out loud. At one point in the evening she tried on the yellow satin jacket. It made her feel brave and rakish. He was about the same size as she. He asked to see a picture of her father and she pulled out the photograph album, which naturally led to his telling stories about his family. It seemed to her at first that he had grown up in a house with twenty-seven people. Later in the evening she realized that some of those people had died before he was born, and some were only hazy boyhood memories fleshed out by family mythology. He lived in a kind of elastic time line; these people were all present, familiar, and vital to him.

He was careful not to allude to his love life at all, and she was careful not to ask anything about Harold. Finally, yawning irrepressibly, both looking pale and rumpled, they said good night. He insisted she keep the leftovers. She watched him get into the elevator, reading the small print on his back. *One Never Knows, Do One?* it said. She smiled all the way to sleep.

■ ■ ■

"Hi, Caroline. I just heard about your dad. I'm really sorry."

"Thanks, Peter."

"I thought about the time that Charlie took me to the Princeton Club—when we were engaged, remember?"

She smiled. Peter had been terrified that day. She'd walked him to the club, assuring him that he was dressed all right, that nobody at the club would care where he'd gone to school, that her father just wanted to introduce him around. He was white as a sheet when he left her at the corner. "I remember."

"I think I loved him."

She swallowed. "He was pretty lovable, all in all."

"He was." He sounded like the Peter she'd managed to forget—the eager, unsophisticated boy who'd promised to take her to the *Nutcracker* every Christmas as long as they lived. She sat holding the receiver lightly against her face, waiting. "He really was. Incidentally, I was sorry that I had to hear it through the grapevine. I wish you'd called us. We'd have wanted to come to the wake."

Ah, you and the little wife. That would have been sweet. She sat up straight. "There was no wake. They recovered the bodies—some of them, anyway—but they're holding them for the investigation."

"No wake? For Charlie Mayhew? Hey, body or no, if there ever was a guy who'd have wanted a wake—"

THE GRACEFUL EXIT

"You have a drink in his memory, Peter. You and Kate."
"Kate isn't drinking these days. You know she's—"
"Pregnant. Of course. Well, you have a scotch and Kate can have a glass of milk. Charlie would have been so touched."

She yanked the door of her closet open; it hit the wall with a bang. She pulled a khaki skirt over her head, and a khaki and white sweater she'd bought on sale, regretted, and never worn. She drove to work, too fast, hating Peter. Between Rye and Port Chester she relented for a moment. That parting remark was a mean thing to say. Too mean and too sarcastic. He'd been kind to call, after all. Maybe she ought to call him back and set it right. She considered it for a minute. No, the truth was, he probably hadn't even heard the sarcasm. Peter could be very dense. In fact, it was pretty stupid of him to talk about bringing Kate to the wake. Stupid and dense. Classic Peter. She leaned into the wheel and picked up speed again, seething. She hadn't been nasty enough, that was the truth. When he said, "I think I loved him," she should have said, "You'll get over it. You thought you loved me, too." She ran through that scene a couple of times, telling Peter off and letting him know that he was never to call her again. It was a glorious scene; she was in icy control, and Peter—Peter was stunned and hurt. At a loss. Finally.

She pulled into Margaret's driveway in a white heat, sliding out of the car in a single, smart sweep as though she were leaving him sitting there, and closing the door with grim finality.

"Get a ticket?"
"What?" She looked around wildly, finally spotting him on the path. Oh God, it was Rob Gerard.
"Your face is flaming red. Did you get caught at the speed trap?"

"No, but I probably should have. I must have been doing eighty." This sweater was an open weave, with strategically placed khaki pockets. She'd let Janet talk her into buying it, but it made her feel like a tart. And here was Chip Charming, who'd practically leapt out of the shrubbery to cross-examine her. Now she really was blushing. Everywhere. She crossed her arms casually in front of her and headed purposefully toward the office.

"You'd better slow down or they'll get you for speeding without a vehicle." He'd caught up with her and now he put a hand on her elbow. "How would you like to put some of that energy into dancing? I promised you a band, remember?"

A whole tangle of feelings assaulted her: Silly, hapless pleasure at being pursued. Annoyance—why hadn't he called, if she was so desirable? Out of sight, out of mind, is that how it was? And envy—he exuded easy charm while she stood rigid and blushing in her ridiculous sweater. And finally, rage, left over from Peter. Damned charming men and their easy, cheap words. And their assumptions. She took a breath, cleared the circuits, and offered him the icy smile she'd meant for Peter. "I can't go dancing," she said in a tone of sweet, triumphant martyrdom she recognized as her mother's. "I'm in mourning."

"Oh Jaysus and Mary, Miss Priss," she heard Charlie howl in his mock brogue from beyond the grave, "don't go blaming it on me if you've a mood on you." She held the door for Rob as he made noises of condolence, then remembered not to extend her arm in the damned, treacherous sweater, and entered the office in a reflexive huddle. Mercifully, there was someone with Margaret. A client, an athletic-looking young woman with black hair in a ponytail, wearing a Polo shirt and a little dirndl skirt and canvas espadrilles. Margaret looked up, clearly alarmed to have her client's privacy violated, but the client seemed unperturbed. She rose and shouldered her pocketbook. "Gotta go. I have to take the girls to riding," she said in a brisk, cheery voice, and smiled at Caroline and Rob. "See you!"

Margaret leaned over to her and said something quietly and they both nodded, then Margaret hustled Rob out of the room toward the library. Before the door had swung closed she was back, looking a little flustered. "Caroline," she said, "this is Ardis. Will you walk her out while I get those papers for Rob? Ardis, I'm so sorry, dear."

Ardis, halfway to the door, waved off Margaret's apologies. "Not to worry," she called back over her shoulder. "God will provide."

This woman didn't require ushering out; Caroline was leaping after Ardis when the back door opened and Sarah stuck her head in. There was nearly a three-way collision. "Oops, sorry!" Sarah said. "I just wanted to ask you to get the house phone if it rings. I'm out here doing garbage retrieval—the raccoons knocked over the cans again."

"That's one problem I've got licked," Ardis said.

"How?" Sarah asked. "They get us once a week. I think we're on their route. I put locks on the lids, too; they're not impressed."

"Forget locks. I set traps," the young woman declared. "I have two of them, one next to the trash cans and one near the faucet. Not only do they not get into my garbage—I take a couple of them out of the game every month."

"You trap them?" Sarah was fascinated. "Then what? The state guy comes and releases them upstate somewhere?"

Ardis smiled sweetly. "That's all I need, another serviceperson to wait for. No, I deal with them myself." She glanced at her watch and evidently decided that she had time to share her raccoon-control secrets. "Here's what you do: once they're in there, you cover the trap. I have some old bathroom carpeting I use, but I guess you could use a plastic dropcloth or a heavy blanket. Then you run a hose from your car's exhaust, under the cover and into the trap. Then you run the engine. Simple." She shrugged in a brisk, self-satisfied way. She thought of herself as a pioneer woman, you could tell. "I use the couple of minutes to do a little weeding. No one does any kind of weeding anymore, no matter what you pay them. Anyway, ten minutes and they're done for."

Sarah was staring at her in fascination. "Mercedes station wagon," she guessed, expressionless.

The woman nodded, already halfway down the driveway. "But it would work with any car," she assured them. They watched her power-walk down the block.

"Oh, how nice," Sarah murmured. "A neighbor. Remind me to try her casserole at the church supper. Ragout of small furry creature, marinated in carbon monoxide."

Caroline stood on the path, watching the young woman as she strode into a driveway up the street, swung into a car—sure enough, a Mercedes station wagon—and tapped the horn two or three times. Two little girls, in jodhpurs and boots, ran from the yard to the car. In a second they were gone.

Margaret was in the office when she returned. "Busy gal, that one," Margaret commented. "Ardis runs half the town."

"Who's the Beneficiary?" Caroline inquired.

"It would have been her mother. Poor thing, she's in sad shape and it's such a burden for Ardis, but we can't do a thing for her."

"Why not?"

"She's in a nursing home. We just can't take a chance when there's an institution involved. I hated to have to say no to Ardis."

"Ardis is a resourceful woman," Caroline said wryly. "I

don't think you need to worry. She'll find a way to deal with her problem." She stood for a moment, considering. "I wonder how big those traps are," she mused.

"Traps?"

"Nothing. Just a little hobby Ardis has that might be useful to her in dealing with her mother. She was telling Sarah and me about it."

"Sarah!" Margaret's brow furrowed. "We have to tighten up around here. First Rob coming face-to-face with a client, and then Sarah . . . it's my fault. I've gotten lax. I'm so used to having you handle the traffic that when I'm alone I'm not vigilant enough. We'll have to—now who's that?"

There was someone rapping at the door. A man, they saw through the window. "That'll probably be the Associated Press, come to take a few photos and do a little profile of our clientele," Margaret said wildly. "Get rid of him."

Caroline opened the door. The man, fiftyish and graying, wearing horn-rimmed glasses and a hat, like a businessman from a fifties movie, smiled cordially. "Margaret Ten Hagen?" he inquired. "Great Events?" Caroline hesitated for a moment. The man, although rather elegantly dressed, looked just like her notion of an IRS agent, or a G-man.

"I'm Margaret Ten Hagen. How can I help you?" Margaret had remained at her desk, and looked at the man with stern authority. Caroline, relieved, moved out of the line of challenge, letting the man enter the office.

"Louis Collier." He took his hat off and stood easily, facing Margaret. He was still smiling. "I'd like to chat with you alone for a few minutes, regarding a matter of mutual interest to both of us." His diction was a little rough; the words sounded as though they were foreign to him. The delivery was formal and slightly menacing.

"Oh, Mr. Collier, I'm afraid we don't accept any clients . . . off the street, as it were. We're by introduction only."

"I'll bet."

Margaret's eyes narrowed and she stood up, preparing to order him out.

"This is in regards to a client of yours," the man went on, unblinking. "Dominick Leone." Caroline recognized the name with a shock. It was that other client of Margaret's who'd been on the doomed flight to London with her father.

"And your association with Mr. Leone?"

"A friend of the family. A close friend. You're busy, Mrs. Ten Hagen, and so am I. If we can have ten minutes alone—"

"This is my partner, Caroline Mayhew. I don't engage in business discussions without her." Collier frowned fleetingly when he heard Caroline's name, seemed to linger on it for a moment, then returned doggedly to his point.

"I think you'll prefer—"

Margaret shook her head, smiling a firm refusal. "What affects one affects us both. Will you have a seat?" She looked at her watch and then, in cool expectation, at Louis Collier.

He shrugged and sat down. Margaret returned to her seat behind the desk. Caroline sat in the chair across from Collier. "I told you, I'm a friend of the family," he said. "I'm a good friend. I'm such a good friend that when I heard that poor Dominick died in the crash"—he crossed himself—"and that it was not an act of nature—"

"Hardly," Margaret interjected.

"—not an act of nature, I took the job upon myself to investigate. Dominick Leone was a very wealthy man, Mrs. Ten Hagen, from a very wealthy and very powerful family. Married to a wonderful girl, three nice kids. And what do I find in my investigation but that he booked this trip through Great Events—very strange, because we have our own travel agent on staff, who takes care of all our arrangements. I find that Great Events is owned and run by a Mrs. Margaret Ten

THE GRACEFUL EXIT

Hagen, a person unknown to anyone in our organization, another strange thing. And stranger still, it comes out that he's left an insurance policy worth a million dollars to that same Mrs. Ten Hagen. Did you know that?"

"He mentioned it," Margaret said, smiling slightly at the memory, "but naturally I didn't believe he'd actually do it—until the policy came in the mail. I was very touched."

"Uh-huh. You were his lady friend, were you?"

Margaret stood up. "You're going to have to leave now, Mr. Collier."

Collier sat unmoving. "A," he said, ticking it off on one finger, "he goes to some travel agent he has no business going to."

"His wife made the arrangements, if you're interested in facts at all."

"Rose did what Dominick told her to do. I told you, she's a wonderful girl. B,"—another finger—"he tells nobody about these arrangements that he makes through this new, strange travel agent, who turns out to be a great-looking woman. Three." Now Collier had three fingers up, pressed together in a rigid phalanx. He shook them slowly and rhythmically at Margaret, like a batonless conductor. "Three. He buys an insurance policy naming as beneficiary this good-looking travel agent, who if Dominick gets to London receives—what? A ten-percent commission?—but who stands to take in a million bucks if the plane has an accident. And what do you know, the plane has an accident, and Dominick dies, and they call it a terrorist incident."

Margaret picked up the telephone receiver. "Get out," she said. She wasn't even breathing heavily.

"Put that down," Louis Collier said in a voice suddenly heavy with menace. He moved slightly on the couch, and the possibility that he was carrying a weapon in his well-tailored jacket vibrated in the room. Margaret stared at him.

"Please," Collier said firmly. Margaret set the receiver down, but kept her hand on it. *I'm going to die in this tacky sweater,* Caroline thought. *Damn you, Janet.* "Thank you," Collier said. "Nobody wants an incident here."

"I imagine," Margaret said coldly, "that you are no stranger to . . . incidents, Mr. Collier. You and your family organization. If you can process the information, I will give *you* three facts. One." She raised a finger in mockery. Her face was just a little rosy now. So that was how she looked when she was enraged, Caroline thought. Or terrified.

"Rose Leone came to me and made arrangements for this trip," Margaret said. "It was special to her and to Dominick. They planned it together—it was Rose's gift to Dominick, who I gather was ill—and they asked for the kind of research and entree that is our hallmark. They got it. Dominick was so delighted with our work that he told me he was going to take out a travel policy in my name. Apparently this was a gesture he'd made before, to other people. Of course his plane never crashed before, so you wouldn't have known of his practice. Actually I didn't place much credence in his promise. Sorry, Louis: that means I didn't really believe him. If I had, I'd have stopped him from doing it. I don't need or want the publicity." She sighed patiently. "Are you following this? All right. Two. When I received the policy in the mail, I wrote a letter through my lawyer to the insurer, assigning my interest in it to Dominick's widow and children. As I said, I was very touched to know that he wanted to thank me in this way, but of course I had no intention of keeping the money. Nor do I need it. A million dollars, after taxes, wouldn't change my life appreciably. And I do pay taxes, Louis, unlike . . . well. To go on: Three." She looked at Caroline. "Other people were lost in that barbaric attack, among them my partner's father."

Collier's eyebrows shot upward. "You recognize the name

now? Mayhew?" Margaret pressed. "Charlie Mayhew was Caroline Mayhew's father. As it happens, Caroline had a very special event planned for her father on his trip abroad, too, one that meant a great deal to both of them. No amount of money would have persuaded me to do anything to destroy that dream. Now I'll ask you to leave."

Collier shook his head blandly. "Oh, no," he said. "It was bright of you to send the lawyer's letter, but I figure you must have been good and scared by then. You're smart. You figured somebody would nail you. And about the other fellow," he nodded sternly at Caroline, "with due respect, you wouldn't be the first girl who had a reason to get rid of her father."

Caroline turned fluorescent pink; she could feel it. "They have the terrorist organization who did it," she said hotly. "Don't you listen to the radio? They even found the bodies, two Arab students—"

"The FAA? They couldn't find a noodle in Chinatown." He got up suddenly, moved to the garden door with startling swiftness, and locked it. He stood where he could cover the interior doors and both of them, and smiled at Margaret. "Now suppose you tell me whose idea this was. One thing I can believe. You didn't need Dominick's million bucks. You came from money, you got money now, and you're always going to have money coming in. So who was it you were fronting for? We don't care about you; you're nobody to us. But we've got wrongs to right, and just now you're in our way."

"Look." Margaret faced him squarely. "I am going to ask you one last time to leave, before I call the police. We have good services here in Greenwich, Louis. The police come like a shot. Maybe you could kill us both before they got here, but I doubt that you want to go to the electric chair for doing a hit man's job. You're a level or two up from that."

It happened so fast, neither of them had a chance to move: Collier's hand moved, the heavy Lucite wastebasket jumped and exploded, parts of it flew up and outward and hit things, there was a tiny pop like distant percussion. Long before either Caroline or Margaret moved, Collier's hand was in his pocket again and the room was still. Caroline, shocked into paralysis, marked the thudding of blood in her chest and ears, took in the fused, distorted base of the wastebasket lying crazily against the file cabinet, plucked at the memory of that distant pop, and noted with wonder the perfect paleness of Margaret's face.

"Rose Leone is my sister," Collier explained reasonably. "Those three orphaned kids are my nephews and my niece. Now, how do I know that someone isn't going to blow up their cars next? How do I know I'm not next? Somebody calls and tells the FAA that the Holy Hoo-Hah Brotherhood of Islam blew up the plane and the FAA is thrilled, they got an answer. Maybe. Or maybe somebody else is responsible, and how am I supposed to sleep at night until I know?"

"I explained to you how I got involved. I told you all I know," Margaret said. Her voice was shaky with emotion— fear, or rage. Or something.

"Explain me again," Collier suggested. "Tell me some more."

Margaret stared hard at Collier for a moment. "Dial your sister's number," she said. "Call Rose. Put me on the phone with her."

He moved so fast, this man. No bouncing, no separate parts flailing at the air. One fluid motion, like skating, and he was at the phone. No one Caroline knew moved like that. *I'll bet he can dance,* she thought hysterically. He punched the number, listened for a minute, then handed the phone to Margaret. Margaret spoke with her eyes on Collier's face. "Rose? It's Margaret, from Great Events . . . Fine, dear. How are you doing? . . . I know. I know. . . . Look, Rose, your brother is here. Louis. Uh-huh. Well, the thing is, I'm afraid that he's threatening my partner and me. He's armed, and he . . . No, but there's been some—unpleasantness. . . . No, no, don't be silly. We can't be responsible for our relatives, God knows. . . .Well it's about Dominick. Louis seems to have it in his head that I'm in cahoots with someone who blew up the plane. . . . Rose, you know that, and I know that, but . . . No, just do one thing for me, will you? Tell him about Dominick's Moment. . . . Yes, the whole thing. . . . No, really, the whole thing. And Rose? I'm so sorry to bother you with this. If there were any other way . . . Thanks." Raising her eyebrows, she handed the phone to Collier.

He listened for a minute, then said, "Rosie, don't talk where you don't understand. . . . Because I am, that's all. Because there has to be . . . Rose, enough. Just tell me what kind of minute she's . . . okay, *moment* . . . " His voice dropped. "No, how was I supposed to know? Did you tell anybody? Benign, you said. You said . . . Oh Jesus." His face contorted in distaste, then his expression slid to horror as he listened. He closed his eyes and shook his head. "Holy Mother," he said. "But then why . . . Yeah, I know, the war, the war, his buddies . . . What, by himself? Yeah . . . To do what? Speak up Rosie, then they were going to do what?" Eyes widening, he stared at Margaret as he listened. "By a *doctor*?" He rubbed a flat hand over his face. "Rose, you were going to *pay* for this? . . . Okay. Okay, honey. Don't cry. Yeah, okay. All right."

He set the phone down, never taking his eyes from Margaret's face. "You're some piece of work," he said. "That's some little cottage industry you got there."

Margaret said nothing. There was an odd look in her eyes, like a cheeky student awaiting acknowledgment of a clever project. "They'll pay anything, right?" he asked. "If they know they're going? A Moment." He shook his head. "But how do they know when to make it? I mean, they could live six more years, right?"

"They're not all sick," Margaret said.

Caroline looked at her in horror. "Margaret—" she began, but Margaret raised one hand: *Leave this to me.*

He considered it. "Suicides," he said, nodding. "It's better for the insurance if it looks like natural."

"No, not just suicides. The point is, our clients don't all arrange it for themselves," Margaret said clearly. "Most don't in fact. Usually the Beneficiaries don't know anything about it. Like Caroline's father. He just thought he was going golfing in Scotland."

She's gone nuts, Caroline thought in despair. Collier was looking at Caroline, aghast. He turned back to Margaret. "Their own parents?" he demanded. "Not their *mothers*."

"More mothers than fathers, in fact," Margaret told him. "For one thing, women live longer. And then, people generally feel that they owe their mothers something special."

"Something special." He was looking a little dazed. "We're talking about death here, right?"

"And beyond." Margaret turned one of her serene smiles on him. "Our service is totally individualized, from beginning to end. Beyond the end, if need be. Caroline was arranging to launch her father's ashes into outer space, for example. Ten thousand dollars to fulfill a lifetime dream."

Now he was staring at Caroline as though she had sprouted fangs. "That's sick," he declared heatedly. "Somebody's got to die, okay. I can see it. But a nice stone, at least."

"Love takes many forms," Margaret said softly. They all stood in silence for a moment.

"So," Caroline said, too heartily. "It was the Arabs after all."

"Yeah, the Arabs." He sighed, quirking his mouth up in exasperation. "Gonna have to deal with them."

"Why? I mean, now you know that no one was after your brother-in-law, right? And the Arabs died in the explosion . . ."

"Two little guys died. The big guy was on the ground. He didn't die in any crash. Are you kidding?"

"But these men are zealots," Margaret broke in. "I mean, they're all willing to die for their cause, so what harm can you—"

"Willing?" he echoed coldly. "They'll beg to die. I've got guys—not these young kids with the briefcases and the telescopic sights, real professionals. Artists. They'd give an arm to do this kind of job. A showpiece, you know? When they get halfway finished, the people who are responsible for that plane crash will crawl the streets begging to die, and anybody who sees them will get the point. The way they'll go, it'll be like the opposite of your deal here. The worst."

Margaret touched a hand to her pearls. "But how will you find them?" she asked. "It's a maze over there, a nest—"

"You ever hear of oil companies?"

"What?"

"You think everybody in the Organization is in Sicily or in Queens? I'll find them."

There was another thoughtful silence. Margaret moved first, tucking a strand of hair back behind her ear and then checking her watch. "Caroline, dear," she said, "I've left poor Rob in the library all this time. Will you see whether he needs anything? Here, take him this—it's last month's records. I was going to get them for him when Mr. Collier arrived."

Mr. Collier. Now he was Mr. Collier again. Caroline left

the office, went directly into the laundry room, and laid her wrists on the cold metal of the washing machine. *A gangster came into the office,* she recited to herself. *A gangster came into the office and accused Margaret of fronting for somebody who blew up the plane. She threatened to call the police and he shot the wastebasket. So then his sister explained to him that she had arranged for Dominick to die some time* after *the plane crash, and he decided not to kill Margaret and me. Then Margaret told him all about her business and now they're in there talking about killing Arabs and Margaret is playing with her pearls and acting like a bride.* She waited a minute to see whether it made sense. It didn't. *A gangster came into the office,* she began again. When she got to Margaret acting like a bride for the second time and it still didn't make any sense, she gave up and headed doggedly for the library. *If Rob Gerard says one cute word to me I'll stab him with the letter opener,* she determined. *And if I ever get home, I'm going to wrap this idiotic sweater around Janet's neck and pull hard.*

Rob Gerard looked up from his orderly spread of papers and smiled. "The rosy dawn," he proclaimed. "Still speeding? Or is that a blush? Ah, you fair-skinned—"

"This is last month's receipts," Caroline announced, holding the folder out at arm's length. "And about . . . about anything else, I can't. I'm in mourning now, and then there are other—"

He held up both hands. "I give up," he said amiably. "No need to explain."

She waited too long, then nodded and retreated. At the door, she turned back to him. "You're very . . . you're fun," she stammered. "And very nice. I just—"

"Hey, don't worry. It wasn't meant to be. Friends forever, though, right?" He winked at her. The whole damn world was winking at her lately. She took a long, ragged breath, then went back to the office.

"I'm an American," Collier was saying. "You don't f— you don't mess with my country, just like you don't mess with my family. You remember with the Ayatollah and the hostages?"

"Of course."

They were sitting on the couch, facing each other like bookends.

"Yeah, well, we offered. The Organization. We said, 'You want to get the job done? Leave it to us.' They wouldn't go for it, though. Democrats got no balls. Sorry, excuse it."

"Don't worry. But then why would they give you permission for this?"

"Permission?" He frowned theatrically. "This is not a question of permission. They went too far for that. This is family now. This is a question of honor. No way I am going to wait around for the pansy State Department to bless this thing. No, no. This is between Louis Collier and some murdering coward. And I'll tell you something: this individual is going to wish he'd never heard of America."

There was a demented, rough grandeur in his attitude. Like some savage king, he sat on the flowered couch, declaiming and shaking his finger, and Margaret, entranced and slightly openmouthed, leaned just a little forward, taking it all in. "He's going to wish," Collier pronounced, "that he'd never been born. He's going to wish that the camel that impregnated his grandmother had never been born. He's going to wish he'd been made without body openings or appendages—especially appendages. And he's going to wish it all over the streets of Tripoli. And if some other would-be terrorist sees him and decides to think twice before he blows up a plane with Americans on it, that's international diplomacy. The kind that works."

Margaret was quite pink now. "Will you go?" she breathed. "Yourself?"

"Sure. This kind of thing, you don't just pick up the phone."

"I want to go, too."

Caroline felt for something solid. The corner of the file cabinet. It was solid and cool and pointed. Good. Cool and pointed was good. Something was very wrong in the world, and if she rested her weight on this cool and pointed solid thing, which felt like reality because it hurt and didn't budge, maybe things would reverse and make sense again.

"No sir," Collier said, apparently unsurprised by Margaret's request. "This isn't for you. Number one, it's dangerous."

"I don't care."

"Dangerous for *me*. Number one, you got a woman along, you give the other side a hold over you. That's just stupid. Number two, *you* are a dead giveaway. You think there's anybody in Tripoli looks like you? Number three, you wouldn't like it. It's filthy there. And hot—you'd sweat. I bet you can't remember the last time you were dirty and sweaty."

"I did field hockey in college."

"Uh-huh. Forget it."

Margaret looked up and noticed Caroline. "Oh, good," she said, "you're back. Listen, can you handle things here for a while."

"A while?"

Margaret looked at her quizzically. "An hour," she chided. "Or two. Lunch. We don't expect anything out of the ordinary, do we? Check the book."

Mrs. Tenant about her lover, the arthritic dance instructor. "Nothing unusual."

"Fine, then. See you soon."

"Bye."

Caroline watched them go, thinking about booking herself on a plane to Pago Pago or Irkutsk or somewhere, but Mrs.

Tenant was due to arrive in half an hour, and then there was the landslide of papers on Margaret's desk to deal with. Filing. The alphabet, at least, was still in place; that struck her as an unexpected bit of divine largess. Caroline began to make order.

■ ■ ■

The May day had turned cool and colorless and they were still arguing. "*Not* to Tripoli, I told you," Margaret said again. "Louis won't let me go to Tripoli. I'm going to wait for him in London. I'll be perfectly safe at the Connaught. What could happen to me in Mayfair?"
"But why?"
Margaret looked at her.
"All right," Caroline conceded. "But why him? Margaret, he's a gangster!"
"Mm." Margaret blinked meditatively. "I think it's because he really has a grip on things." She frowned. "Aside from the bond market, the only thing Mac has had a grip on in fifteen years is his shoelaces." She smiled and patted Caroline's hand, a benediction. "You'll do fine. It's only two weeks."
"In two weeks I could land us both in jail."
"You won't. You're too careful."

■ ■ ■

"So Margaret is at the Connaught, sending down for bath oil and high tea and waiting for Louis to stride back to her bed from his deed of international vengeance, and you are sitting on your corduroy chairpad, alphabetizing the murders. I don't know."
"Would you rather I'd fallen into bed with a Mafioso?"
Janet reflected on it. "Maybe. How's he wear his hair?"

She wasn't kidding. She really wanted to know. When Caroline stared her down, she shrugged. *"And* you slammed the door on Chip Charming for not one single reasonable reason," she persisted. "What was wrong with him? The biggest risk you ran with him was that his calculator would fade in the clinch."

"Somewhere, Janet, there is a man who is neither a Neanderthal nor a con artist."

"And if he decides to murder his wife, you're right there ready for him. Got the field to yourself for two weeks, in fact."

"Pull over, there's a spot."

"Yeah. God, it's pouring. Are we sure we want to see this movie?"

"Come on. We'll run for it."

The coming attractions were blaring as they stumbled over three pairs of legs to seats near the back of the theater. Caroline propped her dripping umbrella against the seat in front of her and wiggled out of her poncho. "What about standards?" she whispered to Janet.

"What about being thirty-five and alone?" Janet retorted. The woman in front of her, about their age, turned around and checked them out without making eye contact. Caroline spied her appraising glance and the hint of a wry smile of recognition. She riveted her eyes on the screen, suddenly terrified to look around, stricken by a vision of the theater filled with row upon row of thirty-five-year-old women with their standards intact and their biological time clocks ticking in relentless unison.

FIFTEEN

IT WAS DIFFERENT, being in charge. She had thought, taking the keys and the calendar from Margaret, that with Margaret gone she would at last have a chance to read through the files, maybe even dig out Dr. Death's identity. Margaret had put as much as possible on hold, vowing that the rest would roll along of its own momentum. But it didn't work out that way.

From the first day, it was as though a playful demon had been let loose on Great Events. The phone was ringing as Caroline let herself into the office at nine on Monday; it was a member of the Enhancement Staff, a cameraman. He was supposed to be leaving Friday to videotape a Moment in Nepal. "You didn't mention a fucking mountain climb, sweetie," he hissed. "Ice picks? Pitons? I don't *do* fucking precipices, love."

"But didn't you know they were trekking?"

"Trekking means *horizontal*. Long, yes. Boring, dirty, trudging along behind some odorous Sherpa, fine. But not up a fucking stone cliff with a sheer drop of God knows how many thousands of feet. Call the Sierra Club, toots. Call Peter fucking Pan and his gossamer wings."

Seven frantic phone calls and three telexes later, she'd found a nonacrophobic photographer who, for a minor fortune, agreed to turn his bar mitzvah booking over to a friend and fly to Nepal to immortalize Beneficiary Furstwangler's last vertical moments.

It was only the beginning. The rodeo they had scheduled for Beneficiary Zabriskie—fairgrounds in Waxahachie, Texas; rental and transport of ten horses; plane, van and hotel reservations for seventy-five invited guests; catered Tex-Mex box lunches and evening barbecue; rodeo master and a dozen and a half attendants—was imperiled by a devastating outbreak of Mr. Zabriskie's hemorrhoids. "He can't even sit to eat dinner without his rubber tube," wailed Mrs. Zabriskie. "How's he going to ride a horse? I think you're going to have to put it off for a week or two. I may have to have him lanced."

Then a congressman who had promised to shepherd a personal bill through the House in commendation of Beneficiary Hogeman's landmark beautification program was indicted for election fraud. While Caroline waited on hold to Washington, D.C., in her fifth frantic attempt to ascertain the status of the bill, she routinely scanned the *Times*'s obituary column and discovered that Beneficiary Wately's mistress had dropped dead, leaving poor Mr. Wately to linger on, unfêted and still impotent, while Great Events got stuck with the outstanding obligations for his farewell ball.

On top of it all, a report came in late on Thursday about the island Sam Ross wanted to rent for Harold's Moment. It wasn't good news. She put the Wately cancellation calls and the Zabriskie hemorrhoids on hold and did an hour and a half's intensive research. Then she called Sam at his office.

"Caroline!" he crowed. "You have no idea what a pleasure this is! Every call I've had today has been a disaster—an assault, a *booby* trap. I was just looking up Witch Doctors in the Yellow Pages—I think I need to have my phone's aura cleaned."

"What's wrong?"

"What's wrong. Whining authors. Manic publisher. Paranoid sub-rights people. Prevaricating agents. Unreliable illustrators with no sense of time or space. An assistant so flaky that . . . well, never mind. A regular day in the lofty halls of the fonts of great literature. So how are you?"

"I've had four days like yours. Worse. And I'm afraid you might need that witch doctor: I'm calling because there's a problem about Harold's Moment."

"No."

"Don't worry; we're going to make it work, but we have hit a snag, and we've got some decisions to make. Could you possibly make one more trip to Connecticut? It's best to do this in person."

"Oh, sure. Why not see if we can decoy the poor schmuck into another death-defying foray into the jungle? Woman, you have no pity."

"I'll meet you at the station with a machete and a fortifying drink."

"Fine, only forget the machete. I don't trust any knife that I can't fold up and fit in my sleeve. And come to think of it, forget meeting me at the station; I'll drive. I remember you on that trip to the station, dropping bread crumbs like Hansel and Gretel so you'd be able to find your way back through the forest. I'm in no mood to be lost forever in Connecticut. But listen, I can't do it tonight. Harold's kind of expecting—"

"Of course. When?"

"What's tomorrow? Friday? If I live through today I'll see you late tomorrow . . . uh, sixish?"

"Tomorrow, at the office."

On Friday, Caroline had lunch with the one new client Margaret had been unable to defer. It was a Mr. Loucas, a novelist; he had insisted that the meeting take place as scheduled. Caroline left the office much too early, afraid she would miss a turn and be late. She arrived at the Petite Auberge twenty minutes ahead of time, frazzled and edgy. She had spent the morning wheedling changes out of recalcitrant reservations clerks and sweet-talking anxious clients, and now she found herself in an evil mood, wishing Beneficiaries Wately, Zabriskie, and Hogeman long, unpleasant lives.

Gary Loucas got to the restaurant fifteen minutes late and out of breath. "I put a call in to my agent at eight-fifteen this morning," he said by way of greeting. "Twelve twenty-four he calls me back. The bastard figured I'd be out to lunch and he could leave a message on the machine and avoid me for another day or two. I know him, though—much better than I ever wanted to, let me tell you—so I waited." He collapsed into a chair, sighing aggrievedly. "They say it's like giving birth, having a book published," he said. "It's true. They fuck you over going in, and it hurts like hell when it comes out. Red wine," he directed the hovering waiter. "Let me see the list."

Caroline, who had been up half the night practicing Margaret-like utterances, didn't have to say a word, as it turned out. She had been afraid that Loucas would try to discuss business over lunch; that wasn't a problem, either. The man, whose novel had been published in March, had a grievance against his publisher that had apparently reached critical mass. It hadn't affected his appetite though; he ate methodically through a prodigious lunch and put away a twenty-four-dollar bottle of burgundy as he recited his complaints nonstop. The publisher, a woman named Sylvie Bremner, had promised him the world. "An important book, she called it. 'A novel of wit and passion—we're really going to get behind it,' she said. I heard it and my editor heard it. She was two hundred percent behind this book. So publication date is March seventeenth, and by April fifth, not one review. My mother's friends are asking questions. *My* friends are crazed. The publishing house does nothing. Not one lousy thing. 'Gee,' they say. 'I wonder why the reviews are so late. We *sent* them the book.' *And* there's no advertising budget. Can you believe that? *And* the one TV interview I get—in Detroit, God help us—they won't pay the plane fare. *And* when I get to Detroit, there are no books. So of course when they try to sell the paperback rights—oh, why go into it? And when my agent finally made his one call to Sylvie, after I went through weeks of agony trying to get him to act alive, do you know what she said?" He contorted his face in a parody of bewildered concern. " 'I don't know *what* happened with that book. I had such hopes for it.' Murder," he proclaimed so loudly that Caroline jumped and looked around in alarm. "Simple murder, that's all. Take a book and kill it."

"Dessert?" she asked, hoping to divert him.

"I can't eat," he said peevishly. "Let's get out of here."

He fell silent and sat wordless in the car, pursing his lips and drumming his fingers on the door handle. When they got to the office, he sat back on the couch and said, "So I'm here to destroy Sylvie Bremner. She has it all sewed up, you know. You can't go over her head at the publishing house—she's sleeping with the head honcho, and besides, she makes them a zillion dollars a year on the one or two pieces of trash she picks out to support. And try getting anyone to print anything against her. Forget it. They're all in the same scratch-me society. So I'm going to kill myself."

He glanced at Caroline, clearly expecting her to react with shock, to try to convince him to reconsider. She regarded him for a moment, her face expressionless. Then she opened the desk drawer, pulled out a lavender legal pad, and began to take notes. "You're doing this yourself," she asked, "or do you prefer that we make the arrangements?"

■ ■ ■

"What good's that going to do him?" Sam Ross asked. He was wandering around the office, investigating.

Margaret would never discuss any client's Moment with another client, but Margaret hadn't had the week Caroline had. Margaret was in London, reclining on a chaise in an ivory nightgown and her pearls, with nothing to do but await the return of her knight from his quest. Margaret didn't trust anybody, either. Caroline trusted Sam. Anyway, she hadn't told him any names.

Gary Loucas had left the details in her hands. "Make it count," he'd said after his communion with Dr. Death. She had no idea how to do that, but here was Sam, put in her path by a providential fate to help her dream up a Moment for a jilted novelist.

"If he kills himself and leaves a note blaming the publisher," she explained, "he figures it will get into the papers and ruin her. No other writers will entrust their books to her, the house will be embarrassed, and so on. He's already written the note—"

"Of course."

"—and what he wants us—me—to do is figure out how to get the biggest exposure. He wants me to hire a public relations person to orchestrate it all, but of course we can't do that. The bottom line is, he doesn't want this hushed up."

Sam grinned at her and shook his head. "I know publishing. If this guy kills himself and blames the publisher, the only effect will be that maybe sales of his book will spike just enough so she gets the credit for bringing in a profit on a low-rent midlist novel. She'll consolidate her power, and the writers will line up at her door."

"He's determined, Sam."

"Hm. Wife and kids?"

"Ex-wife. No kids."

"Well, nobody's going to miss another midlist novelist, except maybe his shrink. And he's probably right; his situation's terminal. He'll write another book and get another identical runaround, so on and so forth, and eventually he'll die of bile and spleen. Might as well check out now and make it count, it shouldn't be a total loss. Let's see."

He lit on the arm of a chair. "Tell him to hold the suicide note," he said after a minute. "Don't leave it around for the police to bury. Let him send it to his agent, to arrive a week after he dies. Then, after the funeral, give him a huge publication party. Invite the regular reporters—you know, not the critics, the news guys. I'll get Harold to toss a few your way. And disclose the suicide note at the party. Make sure you have enough copies of the book on hand. You'll have to pay the publisher for them, incidentally—they might be sorry he died, but they won't be sorry enough to give anything away—so bill your client for them while he's around to pay. Anyway, at the party, pass the word that he was dying of AIDS, and this book was his last chance to be heard. The publisher will look like a creep, and the book will go over the top."

"Why?"

"Why? Are you kidding? AIDS, heartbroken artist, his last expression muzzled? It can't miss."

"You must see so much of it," she murmured sadly.

"What? Crazed authors?"

"AIDS."

He shot a look at her, and she instantly regretted mentioning it. Why did she have to bring it up? Didn't he have enough trouble? She felt the heat in her face and chest.

He shrugged. "I guess the business must have its share. I do hear trees falling out there in the woods. Some good people. Speaking of death, what's the problem about Harold's weekend?"

She'd offended him. Damn. "It's the island," she said. "A developer owns it now. It's kind of built up, and nobody will rent us even a part of it. I've tried everything. Everybody."

He didn't say anything. He stood still as though listening to something.

"Sam? I've been talking to real estate agents in the area. There's an island very much like that one, and we can—"

"Nah."

He hadn't even looked up. Was he going to cancel the whole thing? No Moment for Harold? Her heart sank. She had a ridiculous yearning for Harold to go out in style—entertained, celebrated, and reasonably intact.

"It would be pointless to use a bogus island. Well." He sighed. "Get the boat, then."

"What boat?"

"That was the second choice: charter a riverboat for the weekend, one of those old paddle wheelers with a bunch of staterooms. Red velvet saloon, a couple of pianos, lots of card tables, sleeve garters and eyeshades for everybody. Can you get one with a billiard table?"

"I'll let you know tomorrow. We can always bring one aboard. Where do you want the cruise to go?"

"Do I know? I told you, I don't boat. Just pick a place. Calm. Calm waters. No waves."

"Do you want it staffed?"

"Wenches, you mean?"

"No, I—"

He waved a hand around, dismissing her stammerings. "Let's stay with the original idea," he said. "Just someone to cook, someone to clean up, and tell them to stay out of the way. And a captain, or whoever runs the damn thing. Oh God, I hate boats."

"Then why don't we—"

He shook his head. "So I'll be seasick. I'd be nauseous anyway. This way I'll have a legitimate excuse for it."

They spent the next hour working out the details. They discussed getting hold of a crap table and bringing on a New Orleans jazz band for the Saturday night, and by the time she began typing up the contract, Sam had cheered up considerably.

"How long's that going to take?" he asked suddenly.

"Fifteen minutes. Why?"

"I'm out of smokes, and I really need one. I'm going to run out and get a pack. You'll be done by the time I get back, and we'll get some dinner."

If she'd offended him, he was letting it pass. She smiled gratefully. "Great. Leave the door on the latch—and listen, you go left at the—"

He stopped dramatically in his tracks and raised his eyebrows. "You're giving out directions?"

She grinned; he saluted and left. She had returned happily to her typing when Sarah banged at the office door and leaned in. She was wearing gauzy black Arab pants and a tie-dyed tank top. No bra. "Come on, quick!" she called. "The TV!" She ran off and Caroline followed her.

She'd never seen the upstairs before. It flew past her, a blur of glowing woods, pale silks, and old, soft-colored Oriental rugs. She found Sarah in a big square room with two walls of windows, a fieldstone fireplace, and a big-screen TV.

" . . . to Damascus, where Tim Stoll has the report. Tim?"

"Yes, Jim. What we have here appears to be authentic. It

certainly is extraordinary. I'm not at liberty to say how we got it, but we have very good reason to believe our source, who says that this is the videotaped confession of the person responsible for the recent British Airways disaster, in which three hundred and ninety-one people lost their lives."

"Let me understand. This source was not an official of the police or of any agency?"

"This was a private individual, representing a private organization."

"Tim, that's amazing. Your source agreed to the airing of this tape?"

"Not only agreed, Jim: insisted. Look, Jim, the tape is . . . well, frankly, I hear it's pretty brutal. I haven't viewed it but I'll tell you, those who have are still shaken. It's not for the fainthearted or—"

The anchorman looked directly at the camera. "Viewers, if there are children in the room, you might want to exercise a little parental discretion here. Perhaps—"

"Jim?"

"Yes, Tim?"

"Jim, we've had to black out the video portion of the last segment of the tape—apparently it just couldn't be shown on TV—but of course the audio remains."

"Thank you, Tim. This, then, is the videotape of the British Airways bombing confession, delivered by an unknown source to our affiliate in Damascus, and shown now for the first time."

The anchorman's solemn voice gave way to a hiss and crackle, and the screen suddenly filled with a wobbly shot of wall, floor, table, then of a man sitting on a wooden chair. He wore a sleeveless undershirt and undershorts. His hands and feet were bound. He had a day's growth of beard and he looked haggard. Someone was questioning him in English, which was then translated into Arabic. His responses were translated back into English. The questioner's voice was heavy, menacing; the translator's voice was thin and disinterested, the English clipped and overprecise.

Caroline and Sarah watched as the man first denied, then admitted personal responsibility for the bombing. His voice took on a defiant pride as he denounced the Western powers and began to launch into a diatribe against America in particular. A disembodied hand swiftly appeared, brandishing a stick. "That's a cattle prod!" Sarah exclaimed. The screen went black for a moment, but a shriek could be heard. "You aren't fit to mention the United States of America," the heavy voice declared calmly. "So don't."

It went by like a train in the night, fast and noisy and alternately dark and illuminated. Caroline stared at the screen in wonder, her heart thudding against bone: this man had killed her father. When the screen blacked out, she would put her hands over her ears, anticipating the screams, and senselessly squeeze her eyes shut.

At the end, the man gave up the names of the three leaders of his terrorist group and uttered an apology "to the civilized people of the world." They showed his face as he made his statement. It was shocking; he stared in almost loving, pathetic hope at his questioner. His eyes actually bulged, and his speech was constricted because his mouth was horribly swollen. "Do you swear this?" the heavy voice asked sternly. "On your mother?"

The translation, dispassionate and almost lyrical, followed. There was a surreal stop in the action for the incomprehensible answer, and then the translation: "I swear it."

The disembodied hand appeared again, the screen went blank, and they heard a screaming, pleading voice, then a harsh whining sound, then silence. The American voice said, "This will happen to any individual who perpetrates violence against Americans. This and more." There was a long pause.

"Oh my God." It was Tim's voice, hysterical and shrill. "Oh dear God. You couldn't see it, but what they did to that man was . . . unimaginable. Unimaginable. And then they killed him. Right there in front of your eyes. Right in—"

"Tim? Tim? This is Jim, back in New York. Can you describe how they killed him? Did you see the, uh, the interrogators?"

"No, no faces." Tim was under control again, but his voice sounded wooden. "They used a power saw, Jim."

"A power saw? You mean, to—"

"Right through his face. I tell you, Jim, I never saw anything—"

Caroline ran back through the house and into the office. Hands shaking, she located the number of the Connaught in London, dialed it, and asked to be put through to Margaret.

Margaret's voice sang clearly through the receiver, as though she were in the next room. "Hello," she said pleasantly.

"Margaret? It's me, Caroline. Listen, do you have TV there? I mean, did you see—"

"Of course there's TV. Dear old BBC. This is a *wonderful* hotel: I'd forgotten. The *tone* of the service, the amenities, I—"

"Margaret, there was a transmission from Syria, an—"

"Yes. It turned out to be Damascus instead of Tripoli. Louis was so right. I've never had any desire to be in Damascus."

"But there was a videotape—"

"Yes." Caroline realized belatedly how Margaret's voice sounded. Languid. Contented. You could hear a little smile. "Exciting, wasn't it? So direct. It makes you wonder why our government can't get anything done."

"Margaret, I think that was you-know-who's doing."

"Oh, yes, indeed. Yes, indeed."

"But—it was horrible. Barbaric."

"I suppose. If you were that Arab, I suppose it was rather dreadful. However, now maybe the next overexcited little fellow won't bomb a plane. You know, it was Louis's idea to videotape it for the home audience. He says that the Organization has to make the new technology work for it; why tape a note to a body when there are camcorders? Louis says they showed the whole film in a lot of countries. Every other minute of it was blacked out, here."

"Here, too, thank God. I mean, who would want to see it?"

No answer.

"Margaret? Is he there with you?"

"Uh-huh." There was that creamy, smiling tone again.

"Are you all right?"

"Mm-hmm. Very. Very all right."

"Look, I think you should come right home. Tell him anything, and get out of there. Do you want me to book it?"

"No, no, no. What *is* the matter, Caroline? Are you in some kind of trouble? Is the business—"

"*You* are in some kind of trouble, Margaret! That man is a butcher, and as soon as the video—"

"This man"—Margaret's voice was low and intimate now, really just a murmur—"is an artist." There was a little pause. "Just an artist. I may never come home. I may never leave this room. Except that his business will call, of course."

Caroline crossed her eyes and smacked her forehead with the heel of her hand, like a comic strip character, and just then Sam strolled back in. She raised one finger at him: *Hold on.* "Are you coming home as scheduled?"

"Unfortunately."

"Are you sure it's safe to be with him?"

A chuckle. "Who in the world could be safer? Are you all right? How are things going?"

"One crisis after another," Caroline snapped. "One photographer who defected at the last minute, one Moment delayed due to hemorrhoids, one cancellation with losses to us, one new client."

"Mmmm. Glad I'm here. Look, dear, you ought to relax a little. Everything is taken care of: your father is avenged, and the world is a little safer for democracy. Can't you smile? Smile. See you next week."

Caroline looked balefully at the silenced receiver, then hung it up, shaking her head. "Two more minutes," she told Sam. "Three. I got interrupted."

"No problem, except my extreme hunger. It's pushing seven-thirty."

"Right." Grimly she went back to her typing.

"Hey, you know what?" he said, dropping onto the couch and swinging a leg over the arm. "Your sad sack novelist isn't the only suicide around. I'm driving along listening to the police radio, and I hear all this wrap-up stuff about some woman who just did herself in on a yacht. Listen to what it was called: the *Double Vision*. Is that perfect? It speaks to you of light-headedness, nausea, that exquisite moment of—"

"What? Who did what on the *Double Vision*?"

"A woman," he said patiently, "took her life two or three hours ago on a craft called the *Double Vision*. I love the way they talk on that thing, they said—"

"Shhh!"

"What—"

"Let me think. You're sure it was the *Double Vision*?"

"Could I forget? It made me queasy, just—"

"Hold on a second." She dialed the police, thinking bleakly about canceling another set of arrangements. "Yes, uh, could you tell me, was there a death, a suicide, on a yacht called the *Double Vision*? . . . Me? Just a friend of the family. It *was* the Carr family? . . . Oh, I see. Thank you." Stumped, she tapped one finger on the desk and tried to think what to do.

"I'm sorry. She was a friend of yours? I should have realized—you had that boat . . ."

It took her a second to focus on Sam. "Hm? Oh, no. No. I knew her, if it's who I think it is, but she wasn't a friend." She sighed, exasperated. "I really need to know who it was, though."

"Well, the police'll never tell you. You want to know, I'll find out." He unwound himself from the couch and reached over for the phone. "Hi," he said after a minute. "How you doing? Did you eat? . . . Hey, man, I don't care if you're hungry or you're not hungry. I fixed Bruce's veal and peppers, and you'd better eat. . . . Okay. Listen, I need you to check something out for me. Is Conrad still in Stamford? Call him on the other line; I'll hold. Here's what I need to know . . ."

It was Harold. She felt like a voyeuse. Sam's tone was loving but brusque, not what she'd want in a lover. If she had a lover. If she ever had a lover again. If she ever did anything normal again.

Sam had to repeat everything for Harold, finally feeding it through him to the twice-removed Conrad. He grabbed her lavender legal pad and scribbled on it. "Uh-huh. . . . What time? . . . Uh-huh. Blue. Yup. . . . Oh, *nasty*. Okay, thank Conrad for me. . . . Hey—Harold? Veal and peppers. Now. 'Night. Thanks."

"Okay." He slapped the pad down on the desk. "Here it is: at the Inlet Marina in Norwalk, on the yacht *Double Vision*, approximately, uh, two and a half hours ago, a forty-one-year-old Caucasian female was found dead, an apparent suicide. Asphyxiation. She'd turned on the gas space heater, it seems. She left a note, contents as yet undisclosed, but the signature appears to be in her writing. Name was Patricia Carr, lived right here in—"

"What was she wearing?"

"What? Boy, and they say city folk are obsessed with appearances."

"You said blue."

"*She* was blue."

It couldn't be Trisha. She would never have let herself turn blue in public. "Sam, this is really important. Can you ask Conrad?"

"Conrad gave us his all. That's all there was. Where are you going?"

Caroline went out to the hallway and yelled for Sarah. After a minute, Sarah bounced in. "Wasn't that *wild*?" she demanded. "Why did you run out? You missed the end of it, Tim Reporter torn between the male-ego demand to be this cool professional and the need to vomit. I had a semiotics professor who said that ultimately television and violence would fuse, and it would be a new form. Did you—"

"Sarah, can you do me a really big favor? We have a kind of crisis here, and I need you to do something weird." She turned to Sam. "Could you excuse us for just a minute?"

"Not on your life. Not with a crowbar could you persuade me to leave this room at this juncture."

She had no time to argue with him. Discretion belonged back in that other world, anyway, the one that was rapidly spinning off into the far distance. "Sarah. Take my car and drive to Norwalk, to the waterfront. Find the Inlet Marina."

Behind her, Sam rooted around on the desk until he found the phone book. He dialed and spoke quietly into the phone.

"There will be police there," Caroline went on, "a cordon, maybe. That's why I need you. Marinas are always full of college kids. Maybe they won't notice you. Figure a way to get near the action. A woman died on a yacht. I want to know exactly what she looks like, what she's wearing, what they're saying—whatever you can pick up. Don't tell them your name or anything."

"Dragnet city! What's up?"

"I think the victim is a friend of Margaret's. Listen, can you look preppy? Quickly? So you'll seem like a dockhand or something, kind of blend in?"

"Watch this." Sarah bounced out again, leaving the door open.

Sam handed Caroline a sheet of paper. On it he had written directions to the Inlet Marina. "It's open from the parking lot, no shed to go through or anything. She can walk right onto the docks. The swaying docks." He shuddered. "Better her than me." In response to her puzzled look he said, "Yellow Pages. I called the marina and asked for directions. Said I was Carmichael's Mortuary."

"Harold taught you a thing or two."

"I told you, he tried. I also ordered a pizza. Pepperoni and extra cheese, okay? We're never going to get out of here for dinner. You're going to sit here and wait for Sarah, and that'll be an hour—"

Sarah was back. "I raided Whitney's closet," she said. She had on worn khakis and a green Polo shirt. She wore Docksiders on her bare feet, and her hair was in a ponytail, tied with a green and blue ribbon. She had a Dartmouth sweatshirt tied around her shoulders. It was startling; she looked unmasked.

"Fantastic," Caroline said. "Here are directions, here are the car keys. Go!"

SIXTEEN

SAM'S CONTRACT WAS typed and signed, Caroline had his check, they had finished the pizza and two beers apiece, and still Sarah had not returned. Caroline had tried everything she could think of to get Sam to leave, including the underhanded tactic of playing on his anxiety about leaving Harold alone. It didn't work. Nothing worked. "I'm not going," he announced cheerfully. "Not until I hear what the story is on the blue lady."

She fell back to her second position of defense: decoying him away from probing Margaret's connection with Trisha Carr. She told him about the TV broadcast and the videotape in lurid detail, snaring his horrified attention. Actually it was good, telling it to Sam. He was a rational human being. He reacted appropriately, with shock and horror. He even reached over the pizza box and took her greasy hand in his greasy hand. "One horror on top of another," he said softly. "I'm sorry. You shouldn't have had to see it."

It had been the worst day of the worst week in the second-hardest month of her life. One hot tear, then another, released and slid down alongside her nose. "I never cry in front of anybody," she protested furrily, fighting the babyish downturn of her mouth.

THE GRACEFUL EXIT

"I'm not anybody," he said, and a bizarre surge of feeling sandbagged her. *Oh, swell,* she sneered at herself. *Let's get warm for a guy who's here to arrange the mercy killing of his lover, Harold. Talk about your unrequited love. Talk about pathetic.* It was enough to stop the tears.

She was blowing her nose into a rough paper napkin when Sarah banged at the door and came in. "Do you know that a woman with a rag and a can of polish is invisible?" she demanded. "Nobody even *saw* me. I got varnish on Whitney's khakis, was the only mishap. They had the body on a kind of cot, right there on the dock. Not too pretty." She dangled her arms and threw her head back, eyes closed, jaw slackened, and mouth agape. "Imagine that I'm blue," she said without changing the pose, then straightened up and grinned. "That's about how she looked. Blonde, must have been prettyish. Wearing red shorts and a Mickey Mouse shirt with sequins, can you imagine? Lots of jewelry. They were taking it off and bagging it. She wasn't a real blonde, if that matters, because the hair on her legs was black."

"Did you get a name?" Sam asked.

She nodded. "Patricia Carr, two Rs. The husband was away on business or something, so they'd brought the housekeeper down to identify her. Great type, the housekeeper—glasses on a cord around her neck, white health shoes, kept doing this—" Sarah demonstrated, smacking a flat, open hand on her chest, opening her eyes wide and gasping. "She tried hard to get into the boat to see what was happening. I—"

"Hair on the legs?" Caroline asked.

"Yeah. Well, just stubble, not like mine. Unintentional hair—you know, like she was overdue for a waxing or whatever."

Exactly. She was going to have her legs waxed the day before the Moment.

"Toenails?"

"You are a very sick woman," Sam said admiringly.

"Red. Polish was chipped. Hey, did you know they really do put on a toe tag? I couldn't get close enough to read it."

"Chipped? Huh. What about the boat?"

"Fuzz all over the place."

"Dust?"

"*Cops*. Measuring, taking fingerprints, whatever. Looking officious."

"Where were they doing all this? In the galley or the salon, or in a stateroom?"

Sam shot her a look, head cocked, eyebrows up. *Pretty fancy boat talk*, it said. She shrugged it off.

"In the living room," Sarah said. "All the rest of the boat was kind of closed off with plastic, like the painters had been there. They had the back doors open, so I climbed up from the swim platform with my polish and my rag. I didn't get to see much before they chased me out, though."

"Anything that looked like there'd been a . . . social situation? Champagne bottle, glasses, music going?"

Sarah shrugged. "Not unless you count this month's *Elle* and a solitaire hand. After they shooed me out of the boat, I did try to tune in on her."

"Who?"

"*Patricia*. The sea is pretty good for channeling. I sat on the back of a sailboat and meditated until I got into the blue light, and I tried to call her in, but I didn't get much. If my friend Ved had been there with his oboe, he'd have had her in a second. He raises spirits with music all the time—he's fantastic, much more powerful than me. Want me to call him, actually? It's probably not too late: the spirit usually hangs around the body for hours, unless it's like a truly pure, old soul that zaps right back into the flow. She didn't look real pure to me. She'll probably be stuck to the body for a week."

THE GRACEFUL EXIT

"No, don't bother Ved. I just wanted to be sure it was Margaret's friend, and it seems clear that it was. I'll send flowers and so forth. Thanks, Sarah."

They watched her go in silence. After a minute, Sam silently opened the door and checked the hallway, then closed it again. "Flowers my foot," he declared. "What's up here?"

"No, really, that was what I needed to know. I feel responsible, with Margaret gone. Not too many people know she's . . . on vacation, and Trisha's husband would be hurt if Margaret didn't show up at the funeral or anything . . ."

"My Aunt Ceil used to say, if you can't lie nicely, give it up and settle for the truth; truth is boring, but it always works. Aunt Ceil was a terrific lady and a great liar. *You* are a lousy liar. A person with Belleek-white skin should never try to fool a friend, anyhow; you turn scarlet and—See? There it goes again." He leaned back and locked his hands behind his head, grinning at her, eyes fixed on her eyes.

She picked up the phone book, making a show of looking for Florists, then smiled blandly and brightly at him. "Sam, I really do have to order some flowers and finish up some business here. Thanks so much for—"

He was shaking his head, still smiling broadly. "I brought you this story, remember? The blue lady and her stubble and her chipped toenails, the whole package. I've got a half interest in it. Should I feed it to Harold, or do you want to play nice and share?"

Margaret would narrow her eyes slightly and stare him down coolly. Caroline knew how; she had been watching. She tried it. Sam exploded in laughter. "You look like Wile E. Coyote!" he yelled, pointing.

She could laugh or she could cry. It was a toss-up. She laughed, with tears stinging her eyes. "All right," she said finally, giving up. "You want trouble? Half of trouble?"

"Yup."

Oh, what the hell. She breathed in, blew the breath out. "Okay. That was no suicide. I know this woman, Sam. She'd never *never* have allowed herself to be found with hairy legs and chipped nail polish. Let alone blue skin. And anyway, suicide was the last thing on her mind. She wouldn't have given . . . anybody the satisfaction."

"The police are satisfied that it's suicide. Conrad says: the suicide note was in a sealed envelope and her fingerprints are on the envelope and on the gas heater. There are no signs of a struggle."

"Nevertheless."

They sat in silence for a moment. "Boy," Sam said. "Wouldn't Harold love a whack at this one. One last time."

Caroline looked at the rug and tapped a finger on her lower lip. "Could you be Carmichael's Mortuary again? Call the marina and ask whether the body's still there?"

He dialed and waited, then set the receiver down. "No answer," he said. "I got the machine."

"So maybe everybody's gone. Do you think they left a guard?"

"Oh, no. Wrong. You don't go skulking around the scene of a crime. Especially if it's near water." He thought for a minute. "The husband's not home. You got her home phone number?"

She nodded and flipped through folders until she found it, punched out the numbers and handed the phone to him. It was a relief to have Sam in on this. This was getting scary.

"Carr household? This is Patrick Carmichael, from Carmichael's Funeral Home. If it's possible, I'd like to speak with Mrs. Carr's housekeeper. . . . Oh, you *are*. Wonderful. Miz, uh . . . yes, Miss Novatny. I'm very sorry to bother you, such a difficult day. . . . Yes. No, really? Did they . . . Oh, dear." Sam secured the receiver with his chin and gestured triumphantly, two thumbs up. "Tch . . . Of course you did. Of course . . . No, people rarely do, do they? I wonder, Miss Novatny, could I ask a really difficult thing of you. It's the clothing, Mrs. Carr's interment garb. I tried to think whom to ask, and do you know, I just had a hunch that you would understand better than anyone what Mrs. Carr would want to be wearing . . . Oh, was she? Then she'd be really particular, I suppose. I could ask Mr. Carr, but I didn't want to be bothering him, so painful— . . . Oh, he isn't?" Another thumb jabbed upward at the air. "Perhaps I could stop over there now, then, and spare him the . . . Would that give you time? Well, an outfit, of course, and stockings, shoes . . . Uh-huh. Just use your own fine judgment. Yes. Yesss. Oh, wait, Miss Novatny—the exact address there? That's off . . . Uh-huh, uh-huh. A left and two rights. Ten minutes, then."

He grinned broadly at Caroline. "Novatny's our girl. A born yakker. What do you think, the blue leather dress with the patterned boots, or the new Armani suit she wore to the hospital luncheon?"

"The suit. And check the manicure."

"Quick: what do you want to know? Your one and only chance."

"Why was she on the boat alone? She hated that boat. What got her down there? How long did she expect to be there? And then, what was her mood in the last couple of days—up, down, or sideways?" She looked levelly at him. "Any interesting phone calls in the last couple of days? That's critical."

He saluted. "Gotcha. Wait here; I shall return."

"Oh no you don't. I'm coming with you."

"Morticians don't bring dates on business calls. Besides, Novatny's one of your confidential types; she'll only talk to one at a time."

"I'll stay in the car, then. I'll lie flat in the back seat."

A wicked little smile played over his face. "Do you know,

they all say that. Women just line up and beg: 'Let me lie flat in your back seat.' I have to beat 'em off with a stick.''
"Come on, Sam. This is really important."
"They all say that, too. All right, come on. And don't complain about the back seat—you asked for it."
It was an aging Citroën. The back seat was full of newspapers, steno pads, empty pizza boxes and crumpled McDonald's bags. There was a lingering scent of cigars and aftershave. She liked it. They rode along in silence for a while, and then she said to the ceiling, "She was meeting her husband or a dumpy friend."
"What did you do, raise her spirit with your little kazoo?"
"No, it's simple logic. She would never have let any man except her husband see her looking like that. And no woman friend, either, unless it was a complete frump."
"We'll soon know. Novatny, *j'arrive.*" The car lurched to a stop, the motor cut off, and the door slammed. He was gone. Caroline waited

She woke up in a panic, feeling the car move. It turned, then slid to a stop. The door next to her head opened. "Want to ride up front with the grownups?"
It was Sam. She sat up, trying to catch the tail end of her dream, then flushed as she remembered. It had to do with Sam and the glider in the back yard of her parent's old house, and a long embrace. "What'd she say?" she asked, trying to move briskly to the front seat.
Sam hung something in a garment bag over the back door. "Novatny is a snoop, an eavesdropper, and a gossipmonger. My kind of girl."
"Well?"
"No interesting calls in the last few weeks. Plenty of interesting calls before that, if I caught her drift. Thelma Novatny is no prude, but there was things said on that six-button phone that would make a call girl blush. Nothing she

could repeat to a man, but believe me her, Donahue could have made some show out of it. Although how Miz Carr found time for hanky-panky, what with the decorator and the mass-oor and the shopping, the *shopping*, the things that woman bought—where was I?"

"Hanky-panky."

"Yeah. Not for the last few weeks. At first, after the calls stopped coming, Miz Carr was in the blackest mood, and *mean?*—but then she got contented like, and started going to her exercise class a lot and if you ask Novatny, she should have stuck to exercise all along—you get the same results and no nasty diseases. She, Novatny, never uses any commode in the house except for her own, the one off her room."

"What about the boat?"

"Ah, the boat. Enter the poor schmuck of a husband, bauble in hand. He calls her from the office late this morning. Says he was at the health-care-products show and he stopped to see his friend the wholesale jeweler on Forty-seventh Street. He has a little something for her, wants to give it to her in time for her to put it in the vault before the bank closes at five. So she was supposed to meet him at the boat. I guess the bank was nearby."

"I knew it. I knew she had to be meeting the husband."

"Poor old Novatny went on and on about the space heater. She had a cousin who had a friend whose sister burned to a crisp using one of them things."

"I wonder why it was on the boat."

"Patience, woman; I'm going to tell you. It seems that something was wrong with the thermostat and the air-conditioning ducts in the salon. Can you believe this boat has air conditioning?"

"Absolutely. Don't knock it until you've slept on a sailboat on an August night."

"Or until hell freezes over, whichever comes first. Anyway,

the air-conditioning guru was coming to lay hands on the ducts before the first run of the season. Also, the painters had been there varnishing, so the salon was closed off from the downstairs part. Husband Carr told our lady to bring the check for the air-conditioning man, to sit and wait for him in the salon and not to go anywhere else in the boat because of the wet varnish, and not to touch the windows or the doors. If you get cold, he said, don't turn on the heat—it'll screw up the thermostat. He'd borrowed a space heater from somewhere—said to use that if she got chilly. Novatny said Miz Carr didn't have no business going out in them little short shorts anyhow, and especially not with no head cold like she had. Novatny hasn't had a head cold these thirteen years, but she dresses sensible. And decent. Some doesn't."

"It isn't that cold out. This is June."

"It was rainy, and she was in shorts. Maybe she got cold. Anyhow, her fingerprints are on the heater. Obviously she turned it on."

"Sam?"

"Hm?"

"Could you drive to the boatyard?"

"No sir. No way. Why?"

"I need to see one thing."

"I hate boats and I hate being arrested. Otherwise I'd be glad to help."

She glanced over at him. "If I'm right," she said mildly, "there's a front-page story in this. A byline for Harold."

"Bitch."

"Please."

He drove on in silence. It took her a while to figure out that they were in fact heading for Norwalk.

SEVENTEEN

THE BOATYARD WAS deserted. No one moved on the docks. In a boat at the end of one of the finger piers, there were lights on and music playing. Otherwise the only sound was the one-note chink of stays against masts.

"There's a million boats here! How are you going to find it?" he asked.

She was rooting around in the glove compartment. "It's a Gulfstar 55. Fifty-five feet is big—there won't be many. . . . Does this flashlight work?" She flashed it on and off. It worked. "Are you coming?"

"Do I look like a hero to you? Have a wonderful time. I'll wait here. I certainly hope you don't die."

She sat still.

"What?" he demanded.

"I'm scared."

He shot her a look of pure malevolence, then got out of the car. Grimly, he followed her down to the floating docks. She looked around. "There it is," she whispered. She pointed to a huge yacht at the end of a dock and started toward it.

"Jesus, it looks like a *house*. It's probably locked up tight. Look in the window and let's go."

There was a dock box next to the *Double Vision*. She climbed up it and onto the side deck. She tried the door. It was locked.

"See?" he hissed up at her. "Let's *go*."

She edged along the side of the boat to the aft deck. She looked up at the flybridge. "Come up here," she whispered. "Give me a hand up." After a moment he appeared on the aft deck, looking white and grim. She handed him her shoes. "Give me your hand," she whispered. Leaning hard on his hand, then steadying herself on his shoulder, she climbed onto the steel rail, ignoring the dire warnings he was hissing. Wobbling drastically, she reached for the overhang of the bridge. "Hold me!" she commanded.

He wrapped himself around her, reaching up to her waist. "I'm going to have a heart attack," he reported.

"Not now," she said, heaving herself up onto the bridge, where she disappeared from sight. "Aha!" she said softly, high above him. He heard a sliding sound, then nothing, then a sound at his left ear that made him jump. She stood in front of him, at an open door that led into the salon. "Quick, come in!"

He looked up at the bridge, then at her.

"The hatch up on the bridge was open," she explained.

"Oh. Of course. Why didn't I think of that?"

They were in the salon, a grand room smelling of fresh varnish. The flashlight picked out the peach carpet with a wavy gray swath carved into it. The sofas, set in an L, were peach and gray silk. There were balloon shades of the same fabric, and a gray granite dining table. Beyond the table they could see the pale-peach-stained wooden cabinets of the galley and to the side, blocking the stairwell, heavy sheets of plastic taped to ceiling and walls. Sitting on the carpet next to the glass coffee table, looking dilapidated and out of place, was a pale green enameled metal space heater. Caroline went over to it. "Gas," she said. "This thing must be thirty years old."

"Don't touch it!"

"Don't worry."

"Oh, don't worry. I'm glad you told me. Silly me, I was—hey, where are you going?"

"Engine room."

"Oh my God."

He followed her, protesting in harsh whispers, under the plastic barrier, down the winding stairs, through a little hallway, and into a laundry room. "*A laundry?*" he said in disbelief. She had gone on into a spotless white room, filled with gleaming white machinery. She stood and played the flashlight over the room. "We're looking for the compressor," she explained.

"Oh. Uh-huh."

"Wait, here it is."

"Why didn't you say 'blue box'? I could have found a blue box."

"Aha!"

"What?"

"It's warm."

"Good. Now can we go?"

"The compressor is warm. That means he had the air conditioning running, probably for hours or it wouldn't still be warm. You see? He made the boat cold so she'd have to put the heater on. It must have been freezing up there. It's still cold." She turned the flashlight off. They stood in the gently swaying room, their eyes becoming accustomed to the dark.

"I hate boats," he reminded her. "I'm leaving now."

"Hang on. Would a space heater, even an old one, give off enough carbon monoxide to kill someone in such a big space?"

"How should I know? I was absent that day. Let's go home

and call Con Ed and ask them. Okay? Because—"

She was gone. Panicked, he groped his way out to the hall. Down to the right, he saw the spot of yellow light bouncing around. He followed it. Caroline was in a huge stateroom. She played the light over the king-size bed. "Nobody's been on the bed," she said. "Come on."

She stood still at the top of the stairs, ignoring his escalating suggestions that they leave. "Where do you suppose the chain locker is?" she mused.

"Home. It's probably at home, nice and dry."

"It has to be forward, right? Let's check the forward cabin." She moved purposefully through the galley, under another piece of plastic taped to walls and floor, to a room with a steering wheel and a lot of instruments. "Pilot house," she said. "Pretty fancy." There was another winding stairway at the end of the pilot house. They went down it, Sam protesting vociferously, and into a smaller, V-shaped room. She flashed the light around, picking out a small square door cut into the wall above the bed. She climbed carefully onto the bed and pulled at the little door. It opened, and a rank, metallic smell filled the room. She reached into the opening. He heard clanking. "It's wet!" she exclaimed.

"It's a goddamned *boat*. I keep *telling* you."

"Come on." She closed the little door, slid off the bed, straightened the spread, and led him back up the stairs and through the plastic sheeting. She taped the plastic back down. "The anchor chain was wet," she said. "That means the boat's been out recently. She thought it was still being commissioned for its first trip of the season, but it's already been out." She twisted her mouth. "Wonder where he went," she mused, looking around the pilot house. "If there's a loran . . ."

"A what? Don't touch anything, for God's sake. The damn boat might move."

"A loran. It's just a little navigation computer. Peter had one. The boat isn't going to move. Sit down. I just want to ask it what marks it has."

"A+. Who cares? Let's *go*."

She was pushing buttons on the computer. It hummed to itself and little lights flashed on and off. "It's just like any other computer. Let's see . . . how do I get it to tell me what waypoints he's put into it? Whoops, not that. How about . . . aha!"

"I hate when you say aha. Look, let's—"

" 'Oy Bay.' "

"You said it. Also *gevalt*. We are going to get caught here and—"

"No, it's an abbreviation for a destination, Oyster Bay. Trisha told us that's one of his regular anchorages. Let's see what else. 'L.H.,' that's Lloyd Harbor . . . 'G.Calf'? Oh, Calf Island, off Greenwich. Oyster Bay, Lloyd Harbor, Calf Island—that's it. Trisha said they never went anyplace else. He didn't know enough . . . Wait, what's this? 'P.J.'? Port Jeff! He's got the marks in here for Port Jefferson! What else? 'PtNoPt.' What's that?" She looked around, found a big book, and looked through the index. "Point No Point is off Stratford. That's really a big trip for Leon." She went back to the computer. " 'ExeRok.' Oh God, I remember that one—Execution Rock, that's Manhasset Bay. That's *really* far." She punched the button a couple more times but got no further response. "That's it. Leon had logged in the waypoints for three trips to anchorages an hour or more from here—trips that Trisha didn't know about. And the anchor chain is wet." She turned the computer off.

"The guy had a mistress who liked throwing up," Sam said. "If you'll kindly get us off this damned vessel, I'll explain it all to you."

"He had a mistress and he took her out on long trips on

the boat. And today he turned the air conditioner on and froze the boat so Trisha would have to turn on the space heater to get warm, and she asphyxiated. But that's what I don't understand: did that thing really give off enough carbon monoxide to kill her?"

She wandered into the galley and stood beaming the flashlight around. She opened the oven. "Electric." She checked the cooktop. "Electric. Hm. Wait, what's this?" There was a charcoal grill built into the countertop across from the cooktop. "Aha."

"Oh, shit."

"No, look!"

"I'm looking. What is it?"

"A gas grill. See? These knobs are gas valves." She peered at them, then touched them lightly. "They're off," she said, clearly disappointed. She opened the cabinet beneath the grill and knelt down. "Hey, where's the bottle? These things use gas bottles. We had a gas stove on the Dufour, and that's how it was fed. Peter loved to have a mug of chowder on windy days. It made him feel like an old salt. Every single time I used that stove, he asked me if I'd remembered to close the wheel on top of the gas bottle. He thought I was completely incompetent." She stuck her head under the cabinet. "Here's the line," she said, her voice a little muffled. "It must go . . . " Her voice trailed off as she wriggled farther into the cabinet.

"I'm going now," Sam said. "I'll send the super and you can have a little plumbing chat with him. Bye."

She wiggled back out of the cabinet and sat down on the floor. The flashlight arced crazily around, briefly illuminating her face. She was flushed and frowning. "What? Did you say something?"

"I said good-bye," he said crankily.

She reached up and touched his knee. "I'm sorry, Sam.

We'll go right now. It all makes sense, though, except the gas, and I thought I had that figured out, but all the burners are off and the valves are closed. I wanted to catch him and let Harold break the story. You can't let people get away with murder, can you?"

He turned his head, pulled in his chin and gave her a look. From that great height, the arch of his eyebrows and the tilt of his head were a caricature of irony.

"Okay, but this is different," she protested. "This was *mean*. She shouldn't have gone this way. Blue and . . . I don't know. Exposed. Unready."

"Stubbly. Unpedicured." He nodded, his brow furrowed in mock compassion.

"Everybody has their own ready," she retorted.

He smiled and, taking her hands, pulled her up. "Inelegant, ungrammatical, but accurate. Everybody has their own ready. You're right." He smoothed her hair quickly with his fingertips.

Her face changed suddenly to narrowed watchfulness. "A long lead," she said. "To the bridge, maybe, or out to the deck." She sat back down, swung around, and stuck her head and shoulders back into the cabinet. "Ow." She came out sucking a finger. "Not up," she said. "So it has to go left or right. I'll be right back." Before he could stop her, she had left the room.

He heard a door open. A chill wind blew in. He could hear the tide lapping at the sides of the boat. It was dark. The boat rocked gently on its lines. "Pizza," he remembered uncomfortably. "Extra cheese." He moaned a little.

She was back. "Not starboard," she explained. "Must be port." She patted him. "Right back," she promised.

This time she was gone longer. It was still dark. The boat was still swaying. Sam felt for support. "Starboard," he muttered miserably. "Port. I'm spending the last moments of my life on the ocean, with a female who uses boat words." He shook his head, then thought better of it. "Go get mixed up with Irish women," he told himself, " . . . get what you deserve." He moaned louder than before, a hollow, self-pitying sound.

He saw the moving yellow light before he heard her. "Come on!" she whispered. "We've got to get off this thing!"

He sent her a death-ray look but she didn't see it. She ran to the pilot house, opened and closed a couple of doors, and returned carrying something. She taped the plastic cover back down over the entrance to the pilot house, grabbed his hand, and led him out onto the deck, searching the galley and the salon quickly with the beam, checking the plastic barrier at the stairwell, and then closing the door firmly, quietly behind them. "We're lucky," she whispered. "The dinghy on the next boat is launched. It's just tied onto his swim platform."

He remained icily silent.

They climbed over the rail, onto the dock box, and down onto the dock. It lurched under their feet. They grabbed for each other to steady themselves. "Things are supposed to stand still," he whispered vehemently into her ear. She held onto him a minute longer, to be sure he was steady. "You don't have to come," she said softly. "Don't leave without me, though, okay? Don't leave me here."

"I don't have to come *where*?"

She pointed.

"That?"

She nodded.

"That's a boat, Caroline. Another mother-loving boat, a nasty little rubber one that *bobs*. I *hate* boats. I hate this dock. I want to go—"

"Go!"

"And leave you here? Why do you have—"

"There's no time. Or there may be, but there may not.

He's got to come back tonight, Sam, and we . . . I have to be sure. I have to see him do it before I tell the police."

"Oh, no, you don't. They get paid for this kind of thing; let them do it. Call them up and let's go."

"I can't. Leon might be on his way right now. The police might get here too late, and then no one will ever see him do it. Anyway, I thought this was going to be Harold's story. If I call the police, some local paper will—"

"See Leon do what?"

"Later." She was taking off her shoes and climbing over a sailboat, into the rubber dinghy tied to its stern. "I'm going to untie it. Will you push me off?"

He muttered something and, pulling off his shoes, followed her, slipping and sliding on the varnished decks of the sailboat. Landing precipitously in the dinghy, he clung white-knuckled to the aluminum seat while she pushed away from the sailboat and then paddled ineffectually with one oar. Once adrift, she fitted both oars into the oarlocks and pulled, grunting a little, until they were thirty or forty feet out into the harbor, drifting behind a trawler that bobbed on its mooring. She maneuvered close to the trawler and tied the dinghy loosely to its swim platform. It got very quiet.

"Rolly tonight," she said faintly at last. "It's usually so calm at night. I guess it's the wind, all that rain . . . "

Nothing.

"Well, you didn't have to come," she said. "Why did you?"

His voice, in the starless night, was grim and controlled, if a little shaky. "I'll draw you a picture sometime," he said. "Meanwhile, will you very kindly explain to me what we are doing sitting out here in this . . . thing, in the cold, in the goddamn Atlantic Ocean?"

"The Sound."

"Well?"

"We're waiting for Leon. He's got to come, Sam. He left the gas on and he'll have to come back to turn it off. See, that's why we're here at this angle. We can see the port side of the *Double Vision* from here."

"What are you talking about?"

"Leon told Trisha to meet him at the boat before five, right?"

"Right."

"And he turned the air conditioner on high a long time before she got there. Maybe he had it on a timer, I don't know. Anyhow it must have been freezing in there, so she turned the heater on. God knows where he had to go to find that old gas heater." She shivered. "Poor Trisha. Anyhow, he's had some varnishing done and the salon and galley are blocked off with plastic. Probably the varnish and her head cold kept her from smelling the gas. Now she turns the heater on, so her fingerprints are on it, right?"

He nodded.

"And when the police get there, the air conditioner is off, the room has been warmed by the heater, the cabin is sealed closed, there's a smell of gas, and her prints—*her* prints only, I suppose—are on the dial of the gas heater and on the envelope that has the suicide note in it." She paused for a moment, distracted by a thought, then put it aside and went on. "No signs of a struggle, no reason to doubt anything. I mean, the police wouldn't understand about the stubble on her legs."

"I don't know why not. They're Greenwich police, aren't they?"

"Norwalk."

"Oh, of course. That would account for it."

"Shut up. So it's perfect. Except that that little heater would have taken hours to kill her, even if it was really leaky, and she wouldn't have hung around that long. But there was the other gas, from the gas grill. That would have done it. I found the bottle; they'd run a long gas line out through the galley wall and mounted the bottle in a little enclosure on the port deck—for safety, I guess. They turned the gas on and off from out on the deck. So I figure that Leon snuck by outside the boat, probably as soon as she got there, and opened the valve on the gas bottle and let it run. It's open right now. Somehow he must have rigged it so the gas bypassed the burner controls. Trisha said he took a course in plumbing at the Adult School."

"Why didn't we smell gas, then? Why weren't we asphyxiated?"

"I thought about that, and I decided that he must have calculated it so the bottle would run out of gas after an hour or whatever. Anyhow, now he has to turn it off again, in case the police figure it out. If he does come and turn it off, we know we're right and we call Harold and the police."

"Oh, now it's if. *If* he comes?"

"No, I'm sure I'm right. Pretty sure. I brought these from the boat." She showed him a pair of rubber-clad binoculars.

The dinghy bobbed on the choppy water. "When is Margaret getting back?" he inquired.

"Next Saturday. Why?"

"I want to arrange another Great Event." His tone was darkly meaningful. "Maybe she'll give me a quantity discount."

Caroline didn't respond. She sat quietly, concentrating on not shivering. She didn't want to bring it to Sam's attention that it was damp and chilly out on the water, as well as rolly.

"Tell me something," he said.

She waited.

"How did you get into your line of work, catered deaths?

Did you used to throw decapitation parties for your dolls?"

"It's Margaret's business, really. I just joined her recently. I'm actually a real estate agent."

"Oh." He nodded soberly. "That makes sense. Gracious dying, the obvious corollary to suburban life."

She felt miserable. Sam was furious at her; it was cold and she was wearing only linen slacks and a cotton shirt; Leon might not show up for hours. Worst of all, she felt a totally inappropriate yearning toward Sam, deep in her solar plexus. Deep and churning. Or was that—"Ooh." The sound escaped her.

"What?"

"I don't feel so great."

"Oh, don't you dare. Don't you *dare*." He braced her shoulders. She sat tight, quelling all her impulses by main force. "Think of England," he commanded. "Open your eyes. Talk to me. Tell me how you know this Trisha."

Fixing her eyes on his second button, she told him, drawing in deep breaths of cold air between sentences. He laughed aloud at one point, scaring them both. They sat frozen, waiting for alarms and floodlights, but nothing happened. "We're going through all this," he whispered hoarsely, waving accusingly at the dinghy, the trawler, and the waters of the inlet, "to extract justice for the killer of a woman who was going to have herself knocked off in a week? At his expense? In living Kodachrome?"

"Why did I tell you? I'm not supposed to. I'm very discreet—I never tell anybody anything. Why do I keep telling you things?"

"Chickee!"

"What?"

"The cops! Duck."

They huddled down in a bumpy heap, trying to disappear.

THE GRACEFUL EXIT

A wooden dinghy with a small outboard motor cut slowly through the channel. "That's not the cops," she whispered excitedly into his left elbow. "It has no running lights. And it's just one person. That's got to be Leon!" She squirmed sideways and raised the binoculars to her eyes, fiddling with the focus knob. "It's him! He's going right to the *Double Vision!*"

They slowly disentangled themselves and watched as the little boat slid up to the end of the finger pier and stopped. A man tied it up and got out, leaving the engine at a nearly silent idle. In the pale dock lights they could see him. He was pear-shaped, dressed in a business suit. He was carrying something.

"What's he got?" Sam whispered.

"I don't . . . a ladder! It's one of those aluminum . . . There he goes!"

The man was hooking the ladder onto the toerail of the yacht. He climbed it slowly, swung awkwardly over the rail, and knelt on the deck. "Yes!" Caroline exulted. "He's fiddling with the gas bottle! That's it! Wait, what's he . . . "

The port wing door opened, and in a moment their man had disappeared into the boat. The ladder glinted, swaying abandoned in the silence.

Caroline jerked the dinghy's line off the trawler and shoved an oar handle at Sam. "Row!" she said, beginning to pull on her own oar. "Hard!"

They began to turn in a circle.

"Oh, no. Listen—"

"Hurry *up*! Head for the starboard side. *Sam!!*"

"See," he explained, "I come from the Upper West Side. We never—"

She grabbed the oar from him and rowed furiously, pulling them closer to the *Double Vision* despite his mounting insistence that she stop, turn around, let him off, think for just a *second*. . . . She pulled up on the starboard side of the yacht and tied the dinghy to a cleat.

"We're not going in there," Sam proclaimed in a whispered shriek to her back. Too late: she was already hesitating on the first step of the dock box when Sam climbed out of the sharply rolling dinghy after her, landing with one knee on the dock and the other foot hooked desperately around the aluminum seat. "Grandma was right," he keened ardently under his breath. ". . . get mixed up with them . . . trouble . . . *crazy*." He lurched to his feet and looked for her. She was gone. He looked around wildly, then followed her, with bleak fatalism, up the steps of the dock box. He was a corpse; only the formalities remained.

She was crawling rapidly across the deck toward the front of the boat. . . . *kill her*, Sam vowed silently, following her in a miserable crouch. *Forget Great Events . . . do it myself . . . no nice party, nothing.* "What are you doing?" he gasped beside her ear, making her jump.

She pointed. She had come to a stop beside one of the windows on the starboard side of the bow and, rising cautiously to an awkward crouch, had planted the binoculars against the window. She was peering through them. All he could see was a moving spot of light inside the boat. When he focused on it, he realized that it was from a flashlight.

"He's in there, in the galley," she whispered. "It has to be Leon. He just pulled a knob off the grill and put another one in its place." Sam put his nose to the glass and squinted. He saw the man drop something toward his pocket. It missed the pocket and fell to the floor. The man knelt, grimacing, and picked it up, jamming it into the pocket. He was balding. One long piece of hair that had been combed across his forehead swung away like a gate.

"That's the old knob!" Caroline whispered. Sam clamped

a hand over her mouth. He put his mouth against her ear. "Let's go," he said. "Now." Caroline quickly pointed again, then pulled him to the side and down still farther into a crouch. The man was coming forward into the pilot house.

Caroline felt Sam's hand close over her mouth again and his other arm circle her waist, steadying her as she crouched. She straightened slowly, just enough to see into the window. Sam moved with her like a shadow. The man stood in front of a large, square panel. He swept the light slowly over it, found the switch he was looking for, and clicked it downward. He had orange rubber gloves on. Suddenly he doubled over, one hand on his belly. Slowly he straightened halfway up and hobbled toward the interior of the boat, fumbling at his fly with one orange glove. He passed right in front of the window they leaned against. They watched him lift the plastic barrier and disappear down the stairs.

"Irritable bowel syndrome," Sam commented. "Makes perfect sense to me. Now for God's sake let's go before he comes back."

"I'm really sick. But I was right," she said dreamily. She turned and put one hand on his shoulder, pushing herself to her feet. She teetered unsteadily around the bow seat and into the open door. Sam pursued her. He caught up with her in the galley, where she was scrutinizing the gas grill, one hand pressed against her brow. The boat was rocking with the tide, a sort of rolling twist. It registered on Sam that his innards had been aware of this for some time, although terror had temporarily overridden the message. He took her hand. "We're going now," he said feelingly. "We have things to discuss. I have a lot of things to say to you. If we live."

She looked pitiably at him. "Don't be mad," she said thickly.

"You look like a corpse," he said. "And I feel worse than you look. Mad is for well people."

They stood leaning against the cabinets, waiting to regain their equilibrium, swallowing desperately. The wind picked up. Somewhere in the distance a loose hatch banged. Somewhere there was a sound of rushing air. He pulled on her hand. "Come *on*," he said. They turned toward the door. In the doorway facing them, red-faced and openmouthed, pointing a rod of shiny steel at them, was Leon Carr.

EIGHTEEN

HE LAID IT on the counter. "Damn towel rod came off the wall," he said. "I paid the carpenter seventy-five dollars to install the goddamn thing and it comes off in my hand."

He looked into their faces. "You have no idea what a bitch she was," he said simply. He laid the orange gloves on the counter beside the towel rack. "You're the cops, huh?" He sighed. "What did I forget?"

"The valve on the gas bottle," Caroline said, beginning to breathe again. "But it was almost a perfect murder," she added consolingly.

"Yeah, it was, wasn't it?" Leon said with a fleeting proud smile. "Pretty good. You never heard of this one before, did you?"

"No," both Caroline and Sam reassured him at once. "What was the deal with the knob on the grill?" Sam asked.

"Oh, see . . ." Leon patted his pants pockets, brow furrowing, looking for the knob.

"In your jacket pocket," Sam said. "Left side."

"Yeah. Well, now, I don't know how much you know about plumbing, but this is actually—well, they call it a needle valve." He pulled one off the front of the grill. Attached to the knob was a long, slender rod that ended in a fine point. "See? The gas feeds through this ... see how minute that opening is? You can buy them at any plumbing supply place. That valve opens and closes when you turn the knob. The little needle fits into the line and closes off the flow of gas. Turn the knob, the needle retracts, the gas flows through." He shrugged. "I bought one and filed the end off."

"So even if the knob is turned to 'off,' the gas keeps flowing," Sam said.

"Pours right out. It doesn't hurt to die that way." He searched their faces.

"No," they both said. "Right to sleep," Sam added in a tighter voice. He didn't look at all well. Leon laid both valves, the old and the new, on top of the rubber gloves, surrendering the evidence.

"What were you doing at the electrical panel?" Caroline asked.

"Turning off the circuit breaker for the air conditioning. Nobody picked that up yet, did they?"

"Not as far as I know."

"That's going to be some expense," Leon said, evidencing chagrin for the first time. "I just had them varnish all the teak in the cabins below. It's been warm, you know? So when I ran the air conditioner so cold, the fresh varnish crazed all over the damn boat. Four thousand dollars." He shook his head wretchedly. "Now they'll have to strip it down and start all over again. Another four thousand. If I'm lucky."

Caroline and Sam stood silent, in respect for Leon's misery. Finally Caroline spoke, but softly. "How about the note?" she asked. "How did you get Trisha's fingerprints on it without her opening it?"

"When I called, I told her it was the check for the air-conditioning repairman. I told her to bring it to the boat. She would never have opened it; she didn't care how much it was. It was like breathing to her, handing out money. The woman spent like you and I exhale—plenty more where that came from."

Caroline was sorry he had mentioned breathing; aware suddenly of her own, she realized that she was breathing shallowly, quartered between rising queasiness and a tightening in the throat.

"So what are you going to do now?" Leon asked.

Caroline darted a look at Sam. Sam shook his head. "You can't," he said. "What do you tell the police? Who are you? How did you know Trisha well enough to figure it out? Why do you care?"

"You're not the police?" Leon asked.

"Wait a minute," Sam told him.

Caroline turned her back to Leon. "I could call them anonymously," she said to Sam under her breath.

"Who are you, then, if you're not the police?" Leon sounded exercised now.

"*He* could identify *you*." Sam spoke out of the corner of his mouth, *sotto voce*, like a movie thug. "It's too late for an anonymous call. You can't take the chance."

"But what about Harold? This was going to be so terrific for him. One last byline."

"It's just another story. He's probably too far gone to write it anyway. His stuff has been awful lately. Crippled, you know?" Sam closed his eyes and swallowed. He laid his palm against the side of his face, then on his brow.

Caroline turned and shot an appraising look at Leon. He was listening intently. "Who's Harold?" he pleaded. "Who are you?"

They looked at each other. "Private investigators," Sam said. "We, uh, we're not in a position to report this to the police, because of a technicality."

Leon looked warily from one to the other. "You didn't look like cops," he said finally. "But who can tell, these days?" Like someone released from a spell, he listened, testing the silence for a second, and blinked a couple of times, then exhaled briskly, put on the rubber gloves, picked up the new valve, and methodically began to thread it into the gas grill.

"You could turn yourself in," Caroline suggested.

Leon shook his head, frowning judiciously. "I don't think so. I don't feel that guilty, to tell you the truth. Why don't we call it a wash? I never saw you, you never saw me." He put the altered valve in his pocket and walked forward into the pilot house, missing his footing momentarily when the wind hit the boat abeam. "Some wind tonight," he said cheerily.

Sam moaned.

"What should we do now?" Caroline asked in an undertone.

"What should I do," he pondered. He sighed heavily and raised his eyebrows, staring at nothing. "I am either going to propose or throw up," he declared finally. "It could go either way."

"Hey, way to go," Leon applauded from the doorway.

"Propose what?" Caroline asked weakly.

"Uh-oh," Leon said. "A dummy. Just like mine. Look out, man; it's a lifetime of molar grinding. Hee?" He pointed out his back teeth, two neat rows of caps. "The aggravation," he said. "Wears 'em right down."

"Marriage," Sam answered Caroline irritably.

"Marriage?" She rubbed her palm over her face. It didn't clarify anything. "What about your . . . I mean, you're . . . Aren't you . . . What about Harold?"

"Who's *Harold*?" Leon insisted.

THE GRACEFUL EXIT

"His friend," Caroline explained. "His dear friend that he lives with."

Leon nodded, now hopelessly confused. Then he frowned. "You gay?" he asked Sam. "Christ, man, whaddaya gotta bother with a wife for, then? You got it made."

Sam looked at Leon, then Caroline, then Leon. He opened his mouth, then closed it uneasily. Then he ran out the door, leaned over the rail and heaved. Leon shrugged sheepishly at Caroline.

Sam appeared in the doorway, a wad of Kleenex in his hand. "Bathroom?" he asked Leon.

Leon pointed to the stairwell in the pilot house. "Straight ahead at the bottom of the stairs," he said. "Look out for the varnish. And don't lean on the towel rods."

Caroline stepped out onto the deck, drawing in gulps of cold air. When she returned to the galley, Sam was back. "We're going now," he told her. "I'm not gay," he added, looking at Leon. "Not even a little cheerful."

Leon raised his two orange-gloved hands philosophically. "What can you do?" he said. "If you're not, you're not. Well, good luck to you."

■ ■ ■

In the parking lot they leaned against the tires of a yellow crane and concentrated on breathing. "You okay?" Sam asked after a while. She nodded. "No more boats," he told her. She shook her head emphatically: no more boats.

"Can you make it as far as your office?" he asked.

"Oh, sure," she said unconvincingly.

They rolled down the windows of the Citroën. The cold air helped. "Maybe the police will figure it out on their own," she ventured.

"The cops haven't got time to worry about cases that are

already solved," he said. "You thought I was gay? *Why?* I should never have worn that ridiculous jacket. I knew it."

"No, it wasn't the jacket; it was Harold. I mean, you seemed to love him so much. It was really touching, if you want to know. Enviable. And then you were single, living with him, going to concerts and things . . ."

"You were envious? How come?" It was a sulky challenge.

"I wanted somebody to love me that much." Two seconds passed, during which she listened in horror to what she had just said. "Why did I *tell* you that?" she demanded. "I keep telling you things that—"

"Don't you have friends you love? I love Harold—who, by the way, would be falling down laughing at this whole idea. So would his ex-wife, and so would a great many other ladies, including the one she named in court. Where was I? Harold. I love the man. He's a bully and an intellectual snob and he steals my socks and lies about it, but he's been my teacher and my friend since I don't remember when. We moved in together two years ago because—I don't know, because his wife left him and I didn't have one, and it's a whole lot cheaper this way. Also"—he was getting pretty heated now. She tried to interrupt him, but he ran right over her words—"*also,* Harold is more interesting to be with, and less trouble, than most of the women I've dated in the last few years. Don't you have friends like that?"

"Janet."

"Okay. Okay, then." He had both hands on the wheel. His fingers made twin drumrolls. "Boy. This is some interesting fix to be in. What do I do now, give you references? Women who'll tell you everything that's wrong with me, including that I talk too much? I talk too much."

"No. I believe you. I think part of me knew it all along."

"Really? Which part? No, I'm kidding. I'll tell you what

THE GRACEFUL EXIT

let's do now. Let's be quiet for a minute. I'm stopping talking now. Are you still nauseous?"

She took a survey. "No. I think it's gone. I—"

He shushed her with a gesture. They rode on in silence. It was true, the queasiness had passed. In its place, though, was encroaching weariness and an eerie feeling of dislocation, as though something had hurtled past her, turning her around and leaving her facing in a different direction. She closed her eyes, only for a moment.

"Wake up, Tonto. We're here."

They were at Margaret's. Caroline's car still sat, solid and unchanged, in the driveway, as though murders and stealth and seasickness and proposals had never happened. That was possible, too, especially the part about the proposals. Caroline sat thinking it over. She was definitely in a rattling Citroën with Sam Ross, looking out the window at her car. Her feet were definitely wet. That was all she could swear to.

"Are we getting out?" she asked, cagily avoiding any reference to the evening's events.

"*I* am. They had K-Y jelly in the medicine cabinet in the bowels of that boat, and they had a jar of mud masque, facial-hair bleach, four kinds of ulcer medicines and a half-empty Librium prescription, a nasal spray, ear drops, and a package of Dramamine—which is the first and only thing you should have gone looking for on that godforsaken ship of fools. But no mouthwash. So if you'll let me in, I'm going inside to find some mouthwash. I'm in no condition to kiss anybody, as it is."

Aha, she thought muzzily. *He's talking about boats and Dramamine, so it was real. I didn't hallucinate it. And kissing,* she added, following him out of the car. *He's talking about kissing, too.*

"Aaagh," he said. He took off one shoe, then the other, hopping a little. "Wet, squishy shoes," he explained, hobbling across the flagstone path.

* * *

She waited for him to come out of the bathroom, thinking that she ought to call Janet. Instead, she sat in various casual poses on the couch, the chair, the edge of the filing cabinet, and the couch again, feeling ridiculously like the next one up in spin the bottle. The phone rang, sending her hurtling toward the desk in a galvanic sprint. She froze, poised over it, hearing Sarah's flip question: "If just once you didn't answer this phone, would the universe be worse or better?"

A catalogue of the catastrophes that could be assaulting Great Events flew through her brain, faster than light: Beneficiary Zabriskie, now that his entire rodeo had been painstakingly rescheduled, dying inopportunely of impacted hemorrhoids; Trisha's incredibly hung and revealingly dressed porno stud arriving a week early at Leon Carr's threshold together with the video team, satin sheets and studio lights in hand, and colliding on the doorstep with the Norwalk police; Dr. Death calling to announce that he was quitting the business in order to open a chain of drive-in suicide parlors in Southern California.

So she picked up the phone. It was Margaret. "Caroline!" she sang. "Thank God! I tried you at home, and when you didn't answer and didn't answer, I thought you just might be working late."

"What's wrong? Did Louis—"

"Louis is napping. He's just all worn out." There was that purring voice again, bespeaking long hours of sex and room service. Caroline squinched her eyes closed. She actually saw red. Maroon, really, with floating chartreuse spots.

THE GRACEFUL EXIT

"Look, here's the problem. I totally forgot that tomorrow is the annual mother-daughter fashion show and luncheon for the Animal Save-a-Life League."

"I'll call Ardis. She can bring a raccoon."

"What? Caroline?"

"Go ahead."

"Well, it's just that this luncheon's terribly important for us. All the right people go. I've had my seats for ages. Can you save my life and go in my place? Just mention to Kit Sorley that you're in partnership with me, and she'll do the rest. She has one or two people who want to be introduced, and—"

"This is very last-minute."

"Oh, I know, and I feel just terrible. I expect you're probably all booked up, planning something fabulous"—her tone indicated that she expected nothing of the sort—"but this is so important. It's taken me years to get on their list. You could bring a friend."

"What time is it?"

"Noon, at Old Elms. Well, they start cocktails at noon, but if you're there by twelve-thirty, twelve-forty—oh, Caroline, you're an angel. What would I do without you? The tickets are on the bulletin board in the kitchen, along with the raffle stubs. Maybe you'll win the door prize. You are a blessed, blessed person."

Silence.

"How is everything there?" Margaret rolled right on, unperturbed.

"Oh, fine. Except that Trisha Carr killed herself tonight."

"Killed herself? Herself?"

"Yup."

"*Why?*"

"Who knows? Guess she was in a hurry."

"I don't understand it. Where are people's values? Doesn't their word mean anything at all to them? She signed a *contract*."

"Speaking of contracts, how is Louis?"

There was a tiny pause. "Divine," Margaret said the least bit huffily. "Just divine. And you?"

Caroline began to answer, but in the earphone she suddenly heard distant music and, very close, a man's husky voice. Margaret giggled and protested, the sound went flat, then Margaret came back. "Shhh!" she said, stifling laughter. "Caroline?"

"I'd better go, Margaret. I'm in the middle of a crisis here." She hung up. Let Margaret ponder that one awhile. Between couplings and crumpets, let her worry a little.

It was just too much. First a week of total chaos, then that grisly execution on television—which Margaret didn't even find appalling. Good marketing, Caroline supposed she'd call it. Well, no wonder. While Caroline had been fielding all the crises, six fingers in the dike and up to her knees in quicksand, Margaret had been luxuriating in a suite at the Connaught, in bed with Louis the love artist. Anybody would take things calmly after a week of . . .

She kicked her shoes off and cradled her cold, wet toes in her hands. Her linen slacks were terminally wrinkled. How about the last few hours? How about Trisha getting murdered and good old Caroline risking life and limb to catch Leon, all for nothing?

And then for Margaret to call and toss that asinine mother-daughter Animal Save-a-Life luncheon in her lap, assuming that Caroline would have time on her hands on the weekend. What could poor Caroline have to do that was more important than meeting two or three of the right people with dear ones to bump off and the means to do it up in style?

THE GRACEFUL EXIT

Nothing. Naturally. In fact, she suddenly realized something, reeling in sour humiliation: that was the explanation for Sam's sudden proposal, too. Of course. It had to be a joke. She was getting to be that kind of person, the kind that someone would toss off a proposal to just as a joke. Good old poor old Caroline. Pretty funny, huh? "A scream," she said bitterly.

"What?"

Sam stood in the doorway.

"Nothing. Obviously your sense of humor differs from mine."

"On the subject of . . . ?"

"Nothing. Marriage, for one thing."

"Was I joking about marriage?"

"Well, either your remark about proposing was a joke, in which case our senses of humor differ, or it was serious, in which case it was ridiculous. We don't even know each other." She stared at him defiantly, ignoring the creeping heat in her neck and cheeks.

"Hold on there. In the first place, I was dead serious. Near death, but serious. In the second place, did I say when? Did I say a week from Monday?"

"No, but still—"

"Look. I started out editing murder mysteries for a pulp detective magazine. Nobody hates fake suspense more than I do. I figured, let me get the proposal out of the way right up front; then we can relax and see if we like the idea. Although for my part, I already know."

"How can you know? We've never even—"

"One." He raised one hand, folding down his first finger. Instantly she thought of Louis, ticking off his indictment of Margaret, but instead of that dapper, tight, menacing figure, here stood Sam—disheveled, his tie long since discarded, his shirt damp, his pants cuffs wet and his socks sodden. She relented and smiled the slightest bit. Sam frowned.

"One. Intimacy holds no terrors for me. You're never going to look any worse than you did in that kitchen—"

"Galley."

"—in that kitchen, turning alternately fuchsia and mint green, with eyes like fried eggs. Even with gray, frizzled hair and your teeth in a glass, you're bound to look better than you did then.

"Two. No matter what happens, I am never going to hate you any more than I did between the hours of eight-thirty and ten forty-five tonight. So we have the worst behind us.

"Three. You make a nice living, at a business that gives me something terrific to hold over your head when we fight.

"Four. I know for sure that if I marry you I'm not going to end my days in some hideous home for the decrepit—and when I die, I'll at least get a terrific send-off. That in itself is a better deal than most."

She had stopped smiling. She got up and jammed Trisha's file into the middle of the U–Z file drawer and slammed it closed.

"Now what?" Sam demanded.

"I liked it better when you threw up. It was more romantic. You never even said you l— cared for me."

They stared at each other.

"Uh-oh," he said loudly to an invisible audience. "A dummy. Look at me. Do you see Errol Flynn here? This is a person born to be blackboard monitor, a person who's lived his whole life on dry land on the Upper West Side and whose most daring act in his entire existence was to pay a traffic fine with three thousand five hundred pennies. When such a person makes a death-defying leap into a questionable craft on treacherous waters and then leaps out of that craft and onto a floating deathtrap into the arms of a murderer, all in order to keep another person from facing a watery death alone—just what in hell do you think is going on? You think I routinely do this on first dates?"

"I thought you were mad at me, out on the water."

"*Mad* at you? I told you, I *hated* you. But I already knew that I was probably going to marry you. I suspected it when you told me about your cowboy hat that you only wore at home."

"You did?"

He shrugged. "The rest was just filling in the details."

She smiled—a big smile, seeping from the inside out. Brazenly she tipped her chin up a little and caused him to cross the room and kiss her. Big kiss, pulsing from the toes up.

"So how about you?" he asked finally. "It's Friday . . . uh, eleven sixteen p.m. Want to spend the next fifty hours checking me out? Your place. Unless you want to meet Harold."

"I'll meet Harold later. Monday. Sam?"

"Hm?"

"I'd never have you bumped off."

"We have time to negotiate the small stuff. You might not even like me. I might be too charming for you."

"Uh-huh." She frowned. "What does that remind me of? Something I have to do. Something about bumping people off."

"Everything reminds you of bumping people off. . . . *Now* what?"

She'd gone through the office door and into the hallway. She called Sarah. Sarah appeared at the top of the stairs carrying a smoking saucepan and looking frazzled. "The moon must be void-of-course today," she said. "The cat was weird all afternoon and my crystal that I sent out to be purified got cracked in the vat, and now I've burnt the tofu. What's up? Why are you still here?"

"Just cleaning up some things. Listen, would you like to go to a meeting of the Animal Save-a-Life League? It's a luncheon, actually. Tomorrow at noon. Margaret left tickets on the bulletin board."

Sarah frowned.

"You can take a friend. Free wine, open bar."

"Oh, why not? Sure, I guess so. Animal people are always kind of funky. Is it dressy?"

"I think maybe."

"Great. I bought this sari, handwoven by a women's separatist commune in Delhi. It has this incredible border of natural women."

"Natural?"

"Naked. All shapes and sizes. All positions. It's really amazing. I can bring someone?"

It took Caroline a second. She was entranced with the picture of Sarah in her pornographic feminist sari at the luncheon at Old Elms. "Yes. There are two tickets."

"Excellent. I'll bring Ved. He's really into animals. He remembers a lot of his animal incarnations."

"It's, uh, all women, actually."

"That's cool. Ved was a woman in his last life. He can get into it."

Pure evil came over Caroline then. She didn't blink. "Sarah, this is a mother-daughter thing that Margaret always goes to. Will you be sure to send her regrets to everyone? Tell them something—something really big and pressing—called her away, but that she sent you in her place."

"Why don't I tell them I'm her daughter? Would that help?"

Now, I didn't ask her to say that. "Oh—well, yes. I imagine it would. Tell them that."

Sarah went back upstairs and Caroline stood in the darkened

hallway, struggling with her conscience. It was a brief struggle. She emerged grinning and walked back to the office.

"What have you been up to?" Sam asked. He was sitting on the couch, putting his shoes back on over damp socks.

She pulled him up and steered him doorward. "One never knows," she crooned. "Do one?"

RITA KASHNER is the author of two previous novels, *Bed Rest* and *To the Tenth Generation*. She lives in New York.